A

ONE

WOMAN

MAN

A
ONE
WOMAN
MAN

Travis Hunter

ONE WORLD

BALLANTINE BOOKS

NEW YORK

A One World Book
Published by The Random House Publishing Group

ISBN 0-375-50896-1

Text design by JoAnne Metsch

Manufactured in the United States of America

First Edition: June 2004

This book is dedicated to my road dog Willie Martin.

You've always been a One Woman Man.

Thanks for being a friend.

A

ONE

WOMAN

MAN

ARE YOU MY DADDY?

"Are you my daddy?" a soft voice asked. Dallas Dupree felt someone standing over him. He popped up in the bed and looked around the strange room for the speaker. His naked body was covered with sweat.

Where in the hell am I?

Dallas felt someone stir beneath the covers. His heart raced. Joy and fear took over. "Yasmin," he said softly. Then he looked down at the naked woman beside him and jumped. He rubbed his eyes and his head throbbed.

Things started slowly coming back into focus and he promised himself that he'd never take another shot of tequila for as long as he lived.

Last night, he and his coworker Kenya went to Café Intermezzo in downtown Buckhead to have a few drinks. Dallas ordered a round and tried to keep the conversation from venturing too far into his personal life because he wasn't ready to go there. But he knew the inevitable question would come.

Why is a man like you single?

And when it came, he shrugged his shoulders and said, "Don't know."

But he did know and that knowledge hurt like hell. He started throwing back shots of tequila right and left, and before long Kenya didn't exist. Every so often he'd nod his head or grunt, but his mind was on Yasmin. The more he thought about her, the more shots he threw back.

The next thing he remembered was waking up buck naked to a child's voice.

Dallas glanced back at Kenya, who was still sleeping peacefully.

They'd met two weeks ago when she walked into the teacher's lounge at Alonzo Crim High School. He was sitting alone at the lunch table reading a book called *The Pact*, about three young men who made it out of the inner-city projects to become doctors, when Kenya walked in wearing a dress so tight he could see her heart beat. Dallas was convinced that she was a former stripper. He introduced himself and knew within the first thirty minutes of their conversation that she wasn't his cup of tea, but her body—now, that was another story.

Dallas hated the dating scene. All of this bed-hopping and trying to get to know someone was supposed to be over when he found Mrs. Right, but now Mrs. Right was gone and he found himself right back where he'd started. He took a deep breath, stood up and walked into the bathroom. He quickly washed up and then looked around for a towel; when he couldn't find one, he dried himself with some hard toilet tissue, which he was sure she had stolen from the school. He put a pinch of toothpaste on his finger, ran it across his teeth, and rinsed. He looked around the bathroom and grimaced.

She's a filthy li'l something, he thought, looking at urine stains on the floor around the toilet and the dirty bathtub.

Dallas walked back into the bedroom and quickly jumped into his clothes. When he reached down to put on his sandals, he noticed a used condom on the floor beside the bed.

"Aw, damn! Why the hell did I have sex with her?" he mumbled as he picked it up and checked for leaks.

Strange things happen to unattended sperm, he thought, taking the piece of latex back in the bathroom to flush it down the toilet. After he made sure it disappeared down into the swirl of water, he prepared to leave.

He was passing through the living room, which was also messy, when he noticed a little boy with big brown eyes sitting quietly on the sofa with his arms wrapped around his knees. He looked up when he saw Dallas and his eyes showed confusion.

"Hey, li'l fella," Dallas said, surprising himself. He walked over to the little guy.

"Hi," the little boy said cautiously.

"Why are you sitting here in the dark all by yourself?"

"I'm scared," the little boy said in a shaky voice.

"Scared? What are you afraid of?"

"I heard my mommy screaming. Did you hurt her?"

"No, I didn't hurt anyone," Dallas said, wondering if the little guy was talking about Kenya—but she hadn't mentioned that she had a son. "What's your mommy's name?"

"Kenya Latrice Greer."

I've been talking to this chick for two weeks and not once did she mention having a kid. Trifling!

"Your mommy's asleep. Would you like for me to go and wake her up?"

"No. She gets mad when I wake her up."

Dallas knelt down in front of the little boy. "What's your name?"

"Darius Nicholas Greer."

"Well, it's nice to meet you, Mr. Darius Nicholas Greer. How old are you?"

"Four," Darius said, holding up four fingers.

"A'ight, you're a big boy," Dallas said, reaching over to feel Darius's muscles. That got him to smile.

"Are you going to be my new daddy?"

Stunned, Dallas replied, "I'm sure you already have a nice daddy."

"But my mommy told me last night that she was going out with my new daddy," he said, crossing his arms and pouting.

"You know what? It's a little too early for little guys to be up. So why don't you go and crawl in bed with your mom," Dallas said, making a mental note to cuss Kenya out for doing this to her child.

"Okay," Darius said, reaching out for Dallas's hand.

Dallas walked Darius to the bedroom door of the room where just hours before he'd been reintroduced to the freakiness of his past and waited while the youngster snuggled up beside his mom. He waved at the little guy before leaving the house. He knew then that he would never come back.

On the ride back over to his side of town in the West End section of Atlanta, he started thinking about his life and what it had become. With the exception of his daughter Aja, his life was empty. Yes, he could have the company of a different beautiful woman every night of the week, but after they left he would end up feeling just like he felt now—unfulfilled.

Dallas exited off of I-20 at Joseph Lowery and headed toward his house by Clark Atlanta University. He stopped at a red light and took in the grim environment in which he chose to live.

Even at five-thirty in the morning, crackheads, drunks, and all the rest of society's problem children were out in full force getting their hustle on. He furrowed his brows and tried to act like he didn't see the familiar face running up to his truck with a spray bottle of dirty-looking water and some crumpled-up newspaper.

"Can you spare some change? I'm hungry . . ." The guy in the shabby clothes started his speech but stopped when he recognized Dallas. He abruptly dropped the bottle in the street and pulled his left arm up to his face as if he were checking the time. "Where the hell you coming from?"

"What's up, Baldhead?"

Baldhead still looked at his arm as if he were a scolding parent.

"Answer me, boy," Baldhead said, still inspecting his watch-less left arm. "Yo ass out here creeping, ain't cha?"

Dallas didn't answer; he just smiled and shook his head.

"Gotcha self a new truck, huh? What's that, a Cadillac Suburban?" Baldhead said, eyeing the shiny new vehicle.

"Baldhead, you get a job yet?"

"What kind of job I'mma get? Shit, all I know how to do is iron. You know anybody who needs they clothes pressed?"

Dallas laughed. "Can't say I do, Baldhead."

"Dallas, let me hold a li'l sumptin'? A dollar or sumptin'."

"I'm flat broke," Dallas said, showing the palms of his hands.

"Damn, Dallas, you got to be the stingiest rich nigga I know. You buying up all the houses 'round here, gotcha self a brand-new truck, so I know you got some money," Baldhead said as he stepped back and did a little dance. "You ain't think I was up on your business, did you? Boy, I know everything 'round here."

"Then why don't you know how to get a job?"

"Tell your evil-ass brother to give me a job," Baldhead barked.

At the mention of his brother, Dallas bristled. "You tell him," Dallas shot back.

"Hell no. That nigga be done kilt my ass for smoking up all his shit," Baldhead said, smiling and showing off a surprisingly bright smile. "You know Priest ain't used to be that mean when he was a cop. Now he's worse than the devil."

The light turned green.

"Baldhead, I'll see you around," Dallas said, driving off.

Priest, his older brother, had once been a pillar in the community, but he had traded in his police badge for a journey to the other side of the law. The fact that he could do this after the toll drugs had taken on their family ate at Dallas. Their mother died of a drug overdose, their father died of cirrhosis of the liver because he couldn't give up his addiction to the drug called alcohol, and their brother, Antoine, lost his life in an altercation with a small-time drug dealer. Dallas couldn't understand it.

But Dallas owed his life to Priest. At least the Priest he used to know. The Priest walking around now, killing his own people with his poison for profit, was a lost soul. He'd lost his soul when he was fired from the police department for taking money from a drug dealer. After that he stopped caring about his people. When Dallas found out his brother had joined the ranks of the wicked, their bond was forever broken.

But as much as he hated to admit it, he knew it was because of Priest's street reputation that he was allowed to come and go, in the heart of the ghetto, unmolested. Even standing a full six feet three inches and weighing two hundred and forty pounds, he knew someone would eventually try to test him, but it hadn't happened yet, and that could only be the work of Priest Dupree. His big brother was still looking out for him.

Dallas pulled into the driveway of what used to be a crack house. But it looked nothing like it did in the past. Gone were the broken windows, rotting woodwork, and dirt driveway. He had completely gutted the entire place, purchased the lot next door, added on a few more rooms, and manicured the landscape. Now his place looked like it belonged in an exclusive gated community. He pushed the garage-door button and slid his SUV in beside his convertible Lexus.

Dallas walked into his beautifully decorated home and tossed his keys onto his baby grand piano. He took the stairs two at a time and headed straight for his shower. As he removed his clothes the telephone rang.

He checked the caller ID and frowned. It was Kenya. He immediately became aggravated but quickly calmed himself.

Dallas could kick himself about his new predicament with Kenya. He knew she wasn't any different from any other woman; she wanted a man. And since he was nice to her, took her out for dinner and drinks then obviously sexed her up, she felt like she was on the right track to getting one. Wrong! He decided to let the call go to his voice mail.

Even before he went out with her, he knew things would change if they ever had sex. Things always changed.

Dallas wasn't the find 'em, fuck 'em, and flee type. He was more of the find 'em, see if I halfway like 'em, then spend some time with 'em type. He prided himself on not taking people for granted, and when most of his peers were taking full advantage of the disproportionate ratio of women to men in Atlanta, he was proud to call himself a one-woman man. He was always up front and honest, and he tried his best to treat everyone with the same level of respect. It didn't matter if the person was a doctor, a lawyer, or a straight-up hood rat; they all walked in the door with the same value. He especially knew how to treat women, but he rarely ran across a woman who knew how to treat herself.

The minute the phone stopped ringing, his cell phone rang. Dallas shook his head and groaned. "Aww, damn! I gotta stop dealing with these damn stalkers," he said, not even bothering to check who it was.

Another Monday morning was upon him, and he really wasn't looking forward to dealing with a bunch of hardheaded students, petty teachers, and an incompetent principal.

He went into his bathroom and turned on all the jets in his shower. When he had it as hot as he could stand it, he hopped in and let the steam and heat relax him. Ten minutes later he jumped out, dried himself, and took care of the rest of his morning grooming duties.

Dallas walked into his closet and scanned his extensive wardrobe. The way he felt always affected the way he dressed, and today he felt like wearing shorts and a tank top, but if he did, Mrs. Locus, his principal, would have a fit.

For the last few weeks, every morning when it was time to go to work, he started feeling fatigued. *I'm beginning to hate my job,* he thought.

Dallas stood there for a moment and let his newfound reality sink in. He walked over to the window and looked down at the addicts on the corner. Most of them were out prostituting themselves to pay for their habits. He wanted so much more for them, but he shook his head and pulled back the shades.

A simple white shirt and a pair of black pinstriped slacks would do for today. As he dressed, the telephone rang again and he cursed. He walked over and checked the caller ID, and his mood lifted.

"Hello there, little lady," he said, taking a seat on the side of his bed.

"Rise and shine, good-looking. It's time to get up and make the world a better place," Carmen LaCour said to her younger brother.

"I'm tired," Dallas said.

"Well, good morning to you too! Why are you so tired?"

"I don't know." Dallas sighed as he ran his fingers over his closely cropped hair. "Maybe it's my job, maybe not."

"Your job? I can't have the right telephone number. Is this the house of Dallas Dupree?" Carmen said sarcastically.

"Cut it out. I just wanna go someplace where the schools don't have metal detectors. Someplace where the parents take an interest in how their children make out in life. I get so tired of having to do it all myself. I send some parents a note home about their child's behavior and it's never returned. I spend most of my time disciplining rather than teaching. So yes, I'm getting a little tired of it."

Carmen made some sound that meant "I told you so."

"You know, there was a time when teaching was the only thing I wanted to do, but now it just drains me," Dallas said.

"Dallas, honey, I'd be lying if I told you I wasn't sitting over here smiling my face off."

"Come on, Carmen, this isn't funny."

"Change doesn't occur until we get a little uncomfortable. I worry about you over there with those people."

"What do you mean, *those* people?" Dallas said, back on the defensive.

"Just what I said," Carmen snapped. *"Those people."*

"They are *our* people. Black people. And they're human beings just like you and me."

"Humans they are, but they're not like you and me. Those people live by their own set of rules, and one day you'll realize that you can't save those who don't want to be saved, Dallas."

"So what do we do, give up on everybody who does not meet our standard of living?"

"I'm not saying that, but you have to realize the difference between black people and niggers."

"Now, why you gotta go there?"

"You took it there," Carmen said, standing her ground.

"Carmen, it could've been me out on those streets. I just can't be so quick to judge."

"Dallas, I hear you, but it's deeper than you think. You gotta get out of there."

"I just can't become one of those who make good, then run out to the burbs never looking back. I need for my people to see someone up close and personal who is doing something with his life. That way they know they can do it too."

"Dallas, I truly understand how you feel and I commend your effort, but you're fighting a losing battle, sweetie. You're a giver and *those people* are takers. Eventually you'll run out of gifts," Carmen said. "Move, Dallas. If not for you, then do it for Aja. I mean, why wait for one of those animals to hurt your daughter in some kind of drug-induced rage?"

Dallas was quiet.

"I don't have to tell you what an addict will do when he can't get his hands on some drugs. And there you are, flashing all that wealth in their faces."

"I'm not flashing it in their faces. I'm showing them that they can have it too. I'm from here. I grew up with most of these folks."

"Yeah, but that's not what they see. All they see is a man with the means to give them what they need. I'm surprised you've lasted this long without something happening," Carmen said. "Dallas, I want you to come down to the hospital when you get a moment because I want to show you something."

"What?"

"That you're not one of them. Even God said the poor would always be among us. You can't change that. It's divine order."

"I hear ya," Dallas said. It was time to change the subject because neither one of them was going to change the other's mind. "So what's up with you?"

"I'm serious, D.," Carmen said.

"Yeah, I hear ya."

"Maybe you need to take the day off. I got somebody I want you to meet anyway," Carmen said, ready to talk about her favorite subject: finding her baby brother a wife.

"Can't! Got a baby to feed and bills to pay," Dallas said as he stood and cracked his neck to help relieve some of his stress.

"Baby?"

"That's right," Dallas said proudly.

"That's an old woman hiding out in a three-year-old's body. I'm telling you that li'l girl done been here before."

"Pull up."

"I'm just kidding. You know Aja is my heart. Is she up?"

"She's visiting with Yasmin's mom this weekend."

"Oh, that's nice. I know I tell you this all the time, but your big sister is so proud of you."

"Yeah, yeah, yeah," Dallas said.

"Shut up. Now when do you wanna meet this young lady?"

"Never!"

"Dallas, don't be like that."

"Carmen, you know I don't like your bougie-ass friends."

"Now, who might you be talking about?"

"All of 'em."

"You just don't like them because they don't have sex with you on the first date."

"No, cuz most of 'em do. Bougie people are the biggest freaks," Dallas said, cracking himself up.

"Shut up. I can't help it that you're used to dealing with those ghettofied dropouts."

"Whatever! I'd rather deal with someone who knows she needs some help than some educated basket case who thinks she has all the answers just because she graduated from some antiquated school system."

"You're intimidated by a sister's education?"

"Please. Blabbing on about their education is why most of them are single. Then they wanna run around here talking about the brothers ain't stepping up. Whatever!"

"Wrong. Most of my friends are single by choice."

"Yeah, cuz they choose to be bougie and after a brother get that ass he don't wanna deal with 'em."

"See, that's the problem. Brothers always trying to get that ass. Hold on a second," Carmen said as she spoke to her husband in the background.

"Tell pretty boy, I mean Sterling, I said what's up," Dallas said.

"Now, you pull up. Listen, I gotta run but let's talk soon. Have you spoken with Priest?"

"Nope," Dallas snapped.

"You guys still aren't talking?"

"He's my brother and I love him. And I'll leave it at that."

"Okay," Carmen said, deciding not to interfere with their brother thing. She'd learned over the years that they broke up just to make up. "My friend's name is Monique and I'll give her your number. I'll come by on Friday to pick up Aja. Toodles! Love ya! Bye." Carmen hung up before Dallas could respond.

Dallas shook his head and put the phone back on its cradle. He walked by the mirror to give himself a once-over before he left for school. Over his shoulder he saw the reflection of a beautifully framed black-and-white chalked picture of Aja being held by her mother. He'd cried for a week after the artist he'd commissioned to draw it delivered the piece.

Aja was the spitting image of Yasmin. He took a deep breath. Oh, how he missed Yasmin.

2

IN DA CLUB

*D*r. Carmen LaCour walked into her spacious home in the Ashford Dunwoody section of Atlanta and felt as if the weight of the world had been lifted from her large shoulders. After pulling a double shift as the head emergency-room physician at Northside Hospital, Carmen was looking forward to a hot bath and the strong hands of her new husband, Sterling.

Carmen picked up the mail that was stacked on the countertop and thumbed through the bills. She scanned a credit card statement and frowned; too many cash advances. She made a mental note to speak with Sterling about that.

She walked over to the sink and peered out the window into the backyard, where she saw her husband talking with a neighbor. He seemed to be the happiest man in the world, and that made her happy. She tapped on the window and waved. Sterling returned her wave and blew her a kiss. They both laughed at their newlywed moment. It had only been six months since they said "I do," and to her it felt like yesterday. He was a wonderful and delightful man who looked past her size-eighteen figure and saw the true essence of her, and she felt blessed to have him.

Carmen walked into her bedroom and removed her scrubs. She stood in front of the full-length mirror on the closet door and rubbed her hand across her tummy. She had started walking in the mornings before work and thought she could see a little of the results. Carmen pinned her hair up into a bun and walked into the bathroom. She turned on the faucet in their whirlpool bathtub. Just as she started to disrobe, her telephone rang.

"Oh no," she said with a look of disgust at the caller ID. She just didn't have the energy or the patience to deal with Laquita Marie Jenkins, the ghetto fabulous mother of her oldest niece. But instead of leaving a message like a normal person, Laquita just kept on calling. Every four rings, she'd hang up and call back. Carmen was temped to walk around their home and turn off all the ringers, but she was just too tired so she grabbed the remote control and tuned in to her favorite jazz station.

Carmen poured some bath beads into the bathtub and lit a few candles before submerging herself into the soothing water. She laid her head back and tried not to think about the nutcase on the other end of the ringing phone. She pressed the button that turned on the Jacuzzi and smiled as the roar of the motor combined with the soft jazz drowned out the persistent Laquita.

Forty-five minutes later Carmen turned the bubbles off and stepped out of the tub.

Ringgggg. Ringgggg. Ringgggg.

Carmen didn't even bother to dry herself as she stormed over and snatched up the telephone.

"What, Laquita?" she barked.

"Hey, girl," Laquita said as if she were talking to an old friend. "Is Sterling puttin' it down like that or what? I've been callin' yo ass for damn near an hour."

"Laquita, what do you want?" Carmen said, cutting to the chase.

Laquita sucked her teeth. "Well, umm . . . I got some good news, and I got some bad news. The bad news is the department of children's services just left here trippin'. Girl, they talkin' 'bout taking my kids and puttin' 'em in some shelter. You know how some hoes act when they get a little position. Ol' black heifer came up here talkin' down to me."

"So what's the good news?" Carmen said as she held the phone with her shoulder and used both hands to massage her temples. It never took long for Laquita to give her a headache.

"The good news is, you can make good on your promise."

"What promise?" Carmen almost shouted.

"How soon we forget. When your brother died, you said if I ever needed anything, to call on you. Well, damn it I'm callin', and I need for you to keep Kameka. I done had her ass for the last sixteen years and now her daddy's people need to keep her for the next two."

Carmen felt her chest tighten. She loved her niece Kameka, but life in the projects with only negative influences had already taken its toll on the child. Now she was far from the sweet little girl that Carmen had fallen in love with.

"What happened this time, Laquita?"

"You don't even wanna know."

"Yes, I do."

"Kevin's li'l bad ass took some weed to school and got caught. Now they 'bout to send his li'l butt to juvenile. And I ain't trynna have Kameka gettin' taken away on account of what that li'l devil did."

"Where did Kevin get marijuana from? He's what? Eight years old?"

"He nine. You know some kids, just born bad."

"No, I don't know that. What Kevin is, Kevin has learned."

"Well, he damn sure ain't got it from me, cuz I ain't never been in no trouble."

"Who gave Kevin marijuana?"

"Ain't nobody gave it to him. His li'l nosy self went looking through my mattresses and found Bruce's stash."

"Who is Bruce?"

"My man. Girl, he's so fine," Laquita said, smacking her lips as if her mind remembered something sweet. "Nigga got that good hair and he work for the city."

"Laquita," Carmen said, sighing, "what do you need?"

"I already told you. Kameka needs to come and live with you. She can still come and visit me whenever she wants; I'm just trynna keep my baby out of one of them group homes. I been in one and it's a miracle I turned out the way I did."

Carmen would have laughed but she wasn't in the mood.

This girl really thinks she's okay in the head.

Something didn't seem right, she thought. Laquita wasn't telling the whole story.

"Laquita, if I take Kameka, she won't be spending much time over there. We'll be setting up all new ground rules, and I won't have you undoing what I'm trying to do."

"You ain't gettin' no fuss outta me on that one. Hell, I need a break. But you trippin' 'bout the visiting thing. But I ain't saying nuttin, cuz like I said, I need a break."

"A break from what?" Carmen asked, frustrated. "It's not like you *ever* had a job."

"There you go with the hate," Laquita said, popping some chewing gum.

"Trust me, I'm not hating on you. If you're satisfied living like you are, then so be it."

"Living like what?" Laquita asked, clueless. "I'm straight."

Carmen shook her head. "When do you want me to pick Kameka up?"

"Look at you, ha haaah. You all in a rush," Laquita joked.

"Laquita, this is not a game. The courts are threatening to take your children and you still can find some humor in all of this? You really should be ashamed of yourself for putting your kids in this position."

"Hold up, Carmen. I might not have all the smarts you have, but I love my kids and I do the best I can for 'em. So what if I like to smoke my weed and get my drink on? That ain't got shit to do with me raising my kids."

Carmen couldn't believe her ears, but she had been in this same place with Laquita before.

"You know what? I apologize, because you *are* doing the best you can," Carmen said, but the sarcasm went right over Laquita's head.

"You damn right, and cuz like I told that li'l hoe that just left here with the funky attitude, only God can judge me 'bout how I handle mines."

"When would you like for me to pick up my niece?" Carmen said. She figured Laquita was thirty years old and if she hadn't gotten a clue by now then a verbal thrashing from her wasn't going to give her one.

"What about Kevin?" Laquita said, already back to her playfulness. "You know he loves you, too, and I know you don't wanna break up the kids."

"Kevin is not my nephew. Try his father."

"Girl, you know Tyrone is ghetto. If I send Kevin over there I might as well ask the judge to keep him locked up, cuz he'll end up killing some damn body."

Carmen sighed. *Unbelievable!*

"I'll pick her up Saturday around noon; please have her ready."

"Damn, you can't come and get her on Friday? 50 Cent's in town."

"Who?"

"You don't know who 50 Cent is?"

"No!"

"You can find me in da club, bottle fulla bub," Laquita starting singing. "That's the jam, girl."

"Laquita, I'll see you on Saturday," Carmen said slowly.

"A'ight, Carmen," Laquita said before hanging up.

Carmen placed the phone on its cradle and stared at it as if it were crazy—as if she were looking at Laquita.

That chick has some serious issues.

Carmen was sitting on the edge of the bed when Sterling walked in.

"How's the love of my life doing today?" he said.

"Not too good," Carmen said, thinking about what she'd just agreed to do.

"What's wrong?" Sterling said, sitting down beside her.

"Kameka's coming to live with us."

"Oh really?" Sterling said as he raised his eyebrows. "And when did we talk about this?"

"We need to talk about it now."

"It seems like you've already made the decision. So what good is talking after the fact?"

Carmen ran her fingers through her hair. "I have to do this. She's family."

"And what about Dallas? What about Priest?"

"You know Dallas has his hands full with Aja, and Priest . . . well, he's just not an option."

"I guess you've got it all figured out, Carmen," Sterling said as he stood, threw up his hands, and stalked out of the room.

3

MY YESTERDAY

*D*allas sat in his driveway, unable to move. His mind was on Yasmin and how shallow his life was without her. After she went away, it took him two and a half years before he could allow himself to enjoy the company of another woman, and even then it was only to help ease the loneliness. He touched his chest, where there was a small tattooed picture of Yasmin, and thought back to when they first met.

IT WAS Friday night and the Shark Bar in downtown Atlanta was packed. They were having open-mike night for aspiring poets, so all of the "conscious" types were roaming the place. Dallas stood at the bar drinking a bottle of water and checking out the smorgasbord of attractive ladies. Then a soulful-looking sister walked over, and all of a sudden he got tunnel vision. She became the only woman in the entire restaurant. She was the color of coal and had slanted brown eyes and the prettiest face he'd ever seen. He knew right away that they would be friends. He didn't say anything, couldn't find the words that would do her justice, so he watched her. Before her, the only women he had found attractive were the light-complexioned, long-hair types, but standing before him, black as a moonless night, her head wrapped in a peach-colored cloth and sporting a tiny diamond in her nose, was truly an act of God.

Dallas's heart rotated in his chest when their eyes met. He couldn't turn away. There was something about her that made him uneasy. Never before had a woman intimidated him with sheer beauty, but he found himself praying she found him attractive. She came a little closer, trying to get the bartender's attention. Dallas could see that she didn't stand a chance with the large crowd, so he decided that was all the opportunity he needed.

"What can I get for you?" he said, nodding toward the bar.

"I just want a bottle of water," she said, easing her way closer to him. "Thanks for helping the vertically challenged." She looked up at him with a smile.

"Not a problem," he said, calling his friend over and ordering her water.

She handed him a five-dollar bill but he waved her off. "It's on me."

"Thank you." She nodded politely.

"Are you reading tonight or just observing?"

"I'm just here," she said, hunching her shoulders. "What about you?"

"Just observing, and I must say, enjoying the hell out of the view." Dallas nodded in her direction, sex oozing from every syllable.

One tilt of her head made him wish he'd never tried that approach. It was as if she were saying, *I see where your head is, and no thanks.*

Her drink arrived and she handed him the money. When he refused it again, she stuck the five in his shirt pocket and walked away.

Dallas couldn't let her leave thinking he was a dog, because that just wasn't the case.

"Excuse me," he said as he caught up to her. "My name is Dallas."

"Nice to meet you, Dallas," she said, looking around the restaurant, unenthused about the tall and strikingly handsome man who had tables of women tapping their friends when he walked by so they too could enjoy the view.

"What's yours?" he asked.

She stopped looking around and stared up at him without speaking.

She only stared at him for a minute but it seemed like an eternity. He was tempted to walk away and chalk her up as just another stuck-up sister who had been hit on one too many times. But something made him stay.

"Ah, I'm not really good at this, umm, this . . ." Dallas fumbled for words.

"Just say what's on your mind," she said, still staring at him.

"I think you're beautiful and I just . . . I don't know. I just wanna get to know you better."

"Why, because you think I'm attractive?"

"Well, you are attractive, but I really like the way you carry yourself."

She smiled and looked into his eyes for signs of game. There weren't any.

"I'm not too fond of the way you carry yourself, Mr. Dallas."

"I know, and forgive me for that. I stepped out of character and, well, I apologize if I offended you."

"It's all good," she said and started looking around again.

"What's your name?" Dallas asked, almost begging.

"It's Yasmin," she said, extending her hand.

Dallas reached out and grabbed her soft hand with both of his. "It's nice to meet you, Yasmin." He liked the way her name sounded leaving his lips.

Yasmin.

"Wanna grab a table?"

"I can't. I'm here with my friends, and I don't want to be rude."

Dallas nodded. Disappointment was written all over his face. "If I gave you my number, would you use it?"

"Are you married?"

"No!" he said, quickly.

"Why'd you say it like that?"

Dallas smiled. "No reason; I'm just not married."

"Any crazy baby Mommas?"

"Nope. No babies either."

"Are you a virgin?" Yasmin said with a straight face.

Dallas frowned at the strange question.

Yasmin waited for an answer, and when there was none she spoke. "So you're the bump-and-dump type, right?"

"No, wrong," Dallas said, starting to tire of the inquisition. "What about you? Are you a virgin?"

"Nope!"

"So how you gonna ask me something crazy like that?"

Yasmin laughed. "I'm just messing with you, man. Calm down."

"Be careful, cuz I'll fight a woman," Dallas said, showing all thirty-two teeth. "Especially a vertically challenged one."

"Don't let the small frame fool you. I pack a mean punch," Yasmin said, making a fist. "Give me your number, because I need to go and find my friends."

"Naw, I don't wanna talk to you no more," Dallas said and walked away but quickly stopped. "I'm just kidding. Gotta pen?"

"Oh, you're crazy for real. Where are you from, Dallas?"

"I'm from Texas but I've been here in the dirty South for a long time. What about you?"

"Seattle, Washington."

"That's good."

"Why is that good?" Yasmin asked, handing him a pen.

"I think when two people get together they should be from different parts of the country. Maybe even different parts of the world."

"Why?"

"So they can enlighten each other. Introduce each other to different ways of life," Dallas said as he wrote his number down on a napkin.

"Aren't you the analytical one. I was just kidding with you earlier, but now I have a serious question."

"Shoot."

"Are you gay?"

Dallas frowned. "Do I look gay?" he asked, offended.

"How does gay look?"

"You know that's the messed-up thing about living in Atlanta. No, I'm not gay, bi, or tri. What about you?"

"Nope, I'm strictly di . . ." Yasmin said and smiled. "I like men and only men."

"Why do women feel a need to ask men that question?"

"Cuz some brothers be creeping on the down low and we don't like those kind of surprises."

"Well, I'm a healthy heterosexual male. I'm not HIV positive. I don't have herpes, gonorrhea, syphilis, or any other sexually transmitted disease."

"That's good to know," Yasmin said.

"Y'all be reading too many E. Lynn Harris books. That Basil guy done messed it up for every damn body."

Yasmin laughed. "I see you've been reading 'em too."

"I read a lot. I thought you had to go?"

"I do, but I'm vibing right now. So, when should I call you, Mr. Dallas Dupree?" Yasmin said, reading the napkin.

"Call me tonight when you get in."

"You sure I won't wake your mother?" Yasmin asked.

"Now you're the one who should just say what's on your mind. I don't live with my mother or my father. I'm grown. Both of my parents are deceased."

"Oh, I'm sorry to hear that," Yasmin said sincerely.

YASMIN CALLED that night and they talked on the telephone until the sun came up. It was as if they were high schoolers. The next day they had lunch, and from that point on they were inseparable. They had what the old people called "good yoke." Six months from the day they met, he proposed. They were all set to live happily ever after. Yasmin became pregnant and their one-bedroom apartment had all of a sudden become too small. Yasmin started having complications from the start of her pregnancy, so Dallas wouldn't allow her to work. But he wanted his family to be comfortable, so even though they were barely making it financially, they decided to move to a larger place. Yasmin struggled through the first two trimesters and they were hopeful that the worst was behind them—but it was only beginning.

One night Dallas came home from a long day of working full time while taking a full load of college courses. When he walked into their apartment, what he saw changed his life forever.

Yasmin lay unconscious in a pool of blood on their kitchen floor.

"Yasmin!" he screamed as he ran over to her. His eyes filled with tears. He checked her neck and found a pulse.

"Thank God," he said.

He picked up the telephone, but it was disconnected.

"Damn it." He cursed his pride for not accepting the money Priest had all but begged him to take. He threw the telephone against the wall, shattering it completely.

Dallas screamed for his neighbors to call 911, but no one heard him. He didn't want to leave his fiancée's side, but he knew he had to get her some help. He forced himself away from her and ran to a neighbor's house to call an ambulance.

Seven hours of extensive surgery later, the doctors delivered a premature but healthy baby girl. Ten days later, Dallas took his family home. Five days after that, Yasmin passed away from hemorrhaging.

DALLAS WIPED his eyes. Every time he thought about Yasmin's short life, he cried. He cried because he knew Yasmin was the perfect woman for him, his soul mate. They fit together like a hand in a glove. He cried because he knew he'd never find another like her. They'd never even had an argument. They'd disagreed, but they could never bring themselves to raise their voices at each other in anger. Every woman before Yasmin and every one after her was nothing but drama. And he cried because he knew Aja would be a better woman if Yasmin were around to raise her.

Dallas wiped his eyes and backed out of his driveway. On his way to school he had this overwhelming urge to talk to Aja, so he pulled out his cell phone and dialed Yasmin's mother's number.

"Hello, Mrs. Gibson, how are you this morning?"

"Tired," Mrs. Gibson said with a chuckle. "Whew, that li'l momma of yours talked me to death last night. I'll tell ya. My daddy this, my daddy that. You got your hands full with that one, I'll tell you that much."

Dallas laughed. "Yeah, she's a ball of fire."

"That she is, but I wouldn't trade her for the world."

"Is she asleep?"

"That li'l momma don't sleep. All she does is nap. We went to bed at twelve o'clock last night and six o'clock this morning, she opening up my eyelids talking about she hungry. Hold on a second. Aja," she called out.

"Daddieeeee," Aja said, excited to hear her dad's voice. "Are you coming to get me?"

"Hey, sweetie. Are you being a good girl?"

"Yes, Grandma bought me my own bed."

"Wow. Now you have two beds. And you're still scared to sleep by yourself," Dallas said, laughing at his daughter.

"Daddy," Aja whined. "I miss you."

"Aw, I miss you too, sweetie, but I have to work today. I'll tell you what. The minute I get off, I'll be over there to pick you up."

"Can you come over for lunch?"

"I'll try. Now I gotta run. I love you. Kiss kiss."

"Mummmmmch." Aja kissed the phone. "See you later, alligator."

"After while, crocodile." Dallas hung up the phone and felt good inside. He loved his little girl, and two days seemed like an eternity when she was away visiting her grandmother.

Dallas pulled into the teacher's parking lot and shook his head. There was a large crowd of students, a sure sign that a fight was in progress. He was back to the hustle. He jumped from his truck and ran over, pushing his way through the crowd and snatching up the participants.

"What's going on here?"

"I'mma kill that punk," one of the combatants said.

"You ain't gone do shit! Ya li'l ho," the other replied.

"Hey. Hey! Both of y'all watch your mouths. Now I thought you guys were cool," Dallas said as he recognized the two. He held both of them by the backs of their shirts.

"Mr. Dupree, he started it. You know I don't mess with nobody," D.J. said. "Nigga mad cuz his girl all on mine. I don't want nuttin to do with her stankin' ass."

Dallas let go of D.J.'s collar and slapped the back of his head. "What did I just tell you about that mouth?"

"Then how come every time I turn around you all up in her face?" Darryl said.

"Both of y'all go to my classroom and wait until I get there," Dallas said as he released their shirts and walked back to his truck to retrieve his bag with today's lesson plans in it.

When he arrived at his classroom, Kenya was sitting on his desk with her legs crossed at the thighs.

Darryl and D.J. were sitting opposite her, laughing and trying to look under her short skirt.

"You two clowns go to class, but I wanna see both of y'all after school. You know y'all should be suspended, don't you? And, Darryl, you don't have but one more time to mess up before you get expelled. Bye."

The boys got up and walked out, both peeking over their shoulders at the shapely legs of Ms. Greer.

"You gonna give these kids a heart attack if you don't find you some longer skirts," he said, taking a quick peek himself before walking behind his desk.

"Man, these ain't no kids. What's up with you?" she asked.

"What do you mean?"

Kenya turned up her lip as if he should know what she was talking about. "You damn near killed me last night. It was like you was in another world. What did I do?" she said, smiling seductively. "And how can I do it again?"

"I don't know what you're talking about," Dallas said, shuffling through some papers.

"Well, let me refresh your mind. You had that big-ass anaconda up in me and you were screwing me like you just got out of some kind of prison."

Dallas didn't respond. He was too busy staring at Mrs. Belle Locus, his principal, who was standing in his doorway listening to Kenya's freaky tales.

"And why didn't you answer the phone this morning when I called? Now that you got the goods you already trying to play me?" Kenya said, oblivious to the fact that they had a visitor. Mrs. Locus shook her head and walked away.

"Will you excuse me for a second?" Dallas said, getting up without waiting on an answer. He ran out of the classroom after Mrs. Locus.

"Mrs. Locus," Dallas called out as he maneuvered his way through throngs of students. "Mrs. Locus."

Belle stopped and turned around to face him. She smiled and acted as if she hadn't heard him calling her. Dallas knew it was an act, performed for the benefit of the many kids walking the corridors. He could see the disappointment in her eyes.

"Hey there, Mr. Dupree, how are you this morning?"

"Can I talk to you for a minute?"

"Sure," she said.

"In private."

"Not right now. I'm pretty busy," she said, as if what she'd heard didn't bother her. "But I'm happy to hear that you're back in the swing of things. Just keep it out of my school," she said matter-of-factly.

Dallas stopped walking. Belle stopped too. They shared an awkward moment of silence.

"You do realize that I have a rule about fraternization, don't you?"

"Yes," he said.

"And you do realize that breaking that rule is grounds for suspension?"

"Yes."

"Okay," Mrs. Locus said. "I'll expect to see you in my office after school."

Dallas nodded his head.

"Belle, I apologize for what you heard, and it won't happen again."

"Good to hear, but I still want to see you after school," she said, turning on her heels and storming off down the corridor.

Dallas shook his head to clear the drama and looked up to the ceiling.

Yasmin! I'm trippin' down here!

4

MY PEOPLE

*C*armen pulled her SUV into a parking space in front of the subsidized human warehouses called Carver Homes. She looked around at all the despair and hopelessness and felt a sense of familiarity. To her left was a group of grown men standing around cheering on two pit bull terriers who tried their best to decapitate each other. Music blasted out of the trunk of some souped-up Monte Carlo with chrome rims that spun around even though the car wasn't moving.

Carmen grew up on these same grounds, under these same conditions. She played hopscotch and double Dutch right along with some of the same people who still called Carver Homes their home, yet she still didn't feel safe. She fished around in her purse for her cell phone and dialed Laquita's number.

"Yeah," a deep baritone voice answered, which she

could barely hear over the heavy bass and constant cursing of some screaming rapper.

"May I speak to Kameka?" Carmen yelled.

"She ain't here. Who dis?" the voice said.

"This is her aunt Carmen."

"Okay."

"When do you expect her in?"

"Huh?"

"Will you turn the music down?"

"Hold on," he said, turning the volume down a hair. "I thought you was a bill collector or somebody," he said, then the line went dead.

Carmen sucked her teeth and wished she hadn't changed her mind about picking Kameka up today instead of this weekend. She redialed the number.

"Hello," the same voice answered.

"May I speak to Kameka?"

"Who dis?" he asked again.

"Who is this?"

"This Bruce. You on the way over here to pick Kameka up?"

"Yes."

"Can you stop by a store and pick up some Philly blunts? I'll pay you when you get here."

"No," Carmen snapped.

Bruce didn't respond. He just hung up the phone.

Carmen closed her eyes, took a deep breath, and tried to keep her cool. She got out of the truck and hurried up the walkway between two identical redbrick buildings. She passed a baby wearing a soggy diaper and wondered where his parents were. She turned the corner and noticed about five or six young guys up ahead. As she approached she could sense trouble brewing.

"Damn, you a sexy something. Who you here to see?" one of the youngsters said when he saw her. "I ain't never seen you 'round here. You ain't no P.O., is ya?"

Carmen kept walking until a short stocky kid grabbed her arm. He couldn't have been any older than fifteen.

"Let go of my arm," Carmen said. Her heart was beating through her chest but she didn't let her face betray her fear.

"Damn, Psycho, you better let her go. She's a feisty one," another youngster said.

"Nah, I like mine with a little pepper. What's your name, big momma?" Psycho said, as if he were really trying to gain Carmen's favor.

"I'm going to tell you again. Release my arm," Carmen said, slowly pronouncing each word.

"Or what? I was just trynna talk to your fat ass," Psycho said, roughly pushing her away.

Carmen stumbled back but caught herself before she fell. She adjusted her car keys in her hand until the tiny black bottle was where it needed to be. She looked at Psycho.

"You need to learn some manners."

"Uh-oh, Psycho, you might have to fight," one of the kids said. "And she a heavyweight."

"I got five dollars on the chick," someone else said.

"Gone 'bout yo business, lady. You lucky I ain't take you in the breezeway," he said with a sinister grin as he rubbed his crotch.

Carmen flicked the white safety cap to the side and swung her arm up toward Psycho's face. He froze, staring at the little black bottle as if it were a gun. Before Psycho could duck, close his eyes, or run, Carmen pressed a button, sending a blinding white liquid into his eyes. He screamed like a pig in a slaughterhouse. One of his friends made a move toward her, and he, too, felt a blast of the pepper spray. He yelled louder than Psycho, who was now rolling around on the ground, screaming and holding his eyes. The others laughed as they ducked out of the way of Carmen's sweep.

"Now the next time you see somebody minding their damn business, I suggest you do the same," Carmen said before she calmly walked away. "Bad-ass kids."

When Carmen made it to Laquita's she took her frustrations out on the metal screen door. The door swung open and a man, who Carmen assumed was Bruce, stood before her wearing only a pair of boxer underwear and a dirty doo rag on his head.

"What's up?" he said over the blaring music.

"I'm here to pick up my niece!" Carmen yelled.

"Come on in," he said, unlocking the screen door and stepping back to allow Carmen room to enter. "Yo, did you bring them blunts?"

"Kameka!" Ignoring Bruce, Carmen called out from outside the apartment.

Kameka walked around the corner.

Carmen looked at her and almost couldn't believe her eyes. Kameka looked like a grown woman. It had only been about six months since she'd seen her last, and it seemed like she'd used all of that time to grow breasts and hips. Her resemblance to her brother Antoine was unbelievably strong. They had the same thin lips, high cheekbones, chocolate complexion, and big brown eyes.

"Hey, Aunt Carmen," Kameka said as she opened the door and gave her aunt a hug. "You ready?"

"Yes, are you?"

"Yeah, come on in. I gotta grab my things."

"Sure," Carmen said, hesitating before walking into the humid and cramped living quarters. She stood in the middle of the floor, almost afraid to move. The place reeked of marijuana. "Where's your mom?"

"Sleep. I don't know how with all this loud-ass music," Kameka said, staring at Bruce and turning the radio off.

First thing we do is wash out that mouth, Carmen thought.

"Go and put on some clothes. You see we got company," Kameka barked.

Bruce took a sip of his forty-ounce bottle of beer and slid his hand down his underwear, never even looking Kameka's way.

"You so stupid," Kameka said to Bruce. "Aunt Carmen, I only got one suitcase and I'm bringing my CD player and my CDs, that's all."

"Okay, well, let's get a move on," Carmen said, clapping her hands. "We have a lot to do."

Kameka disappeared around the corner and Carmen stared at Bruce. He appeared to be of some mixed ethnicity but she couldn't be sure. He was handsome, but the one thing she was sure of, without even getting to know him, was that he was a sorry excuse for a man.

Kameka came out of the room rolling a large suitcase and carrying a box. Carmen took the box from her. "You ready?"

"Been ready," Kameka said, rolling her eyes at Bruce.

"Aren't you going to say bye to your mother?"

"Bye," Kameka said, throwing the word over her shoulder before walking out the door pulling her bag behind her.

Carmen noticed Bruce staring at Kameka seductively as he moved his hand around in his underwear. She grimaced and wished she hadn't used up all that Mace.

"Laquita!" Carmen called out.

A few seconds later Laquita appeared wearing only a bathrobe and some house shoes. Her hair was all over her head and her face was puffy from sleep. Laquita wasn't a bad-looking woman. She had a pretty face but could stand to eat a little more; the poor girl was rail thin.

"We're leaving. I'll call you tomorrow to discuss a few things," Carmen said.

"That's cool," Laquita said, looking around the small apartment. "Where's Kameka?"

"She went out to the car."

"Good, cuz I was about to break her damn neck. That mouth gettin' to be just a little too slick. I hope you can teach her some manners."

"I wonder how she could get that way," Carmen said as she stared at Laquita, then at Bruce, with nothing but contempt. "With you guys being such positive role models and all."

"Anyway," Laquita said, sucking her teeth, "I appreciate you taking her."

"I bet you do," Carmen said, tossing a look at Bruce before turning to leave. Before she could get out of the apartment good, she heard the door slam behind her. She was tempted to knock on it and give Laquita a piece of her mind but decided to let it go and walked away.

As Carmen walked back toward her car she saw Kameka talking to the same group of guys she'd just had a confrontation with. When she came up on them they immediately started apologizing.

"I ain't know you was Kameka's aunt. My bad," Psycho said, still rubbing his eyes.

Carmen nodded and grabbed Kameka's arm, never breaking her stride.

They put Kameka's things in the cargo area and buckled up.

"I'm not gonna miss this spot at all," Kameka said, staring back at Carver Homes as they backed out.

"You hungry?" Carmen asked, speeding away from the place she once called home.

"Yeah," Kameka said.

"Kameka, we need to get a few things straight. I need to hear 'ma'am' when you address me. Is that too much to ask?"

Kameka stared at Carmen, trying to gauge her seriousness. "Nah," Kameka said looking out the window.

"Nah, what?"

Kameka didn't respond. She just stared straight ahead. Her mood automatically altered. It was as if laying down a set of rules sucked the life out of her.

"Kameka, I know life hasn't been easy for you. It wasn't all peaches and cream for me either, but I made it through okay and you will too."

"Why don't I know anything about my dad?" Kameka asked softly. "My mom doesn't talk about him, y'all hardly ever come around, and when y'all do all I hear is how much I look like him. That's it."

Carmen was taken aback. She felt guilty for not spending more time with her niece, for not telling her all about her father, for all of the years of neglect.

"I don't know," Carmen said quietly. "I guess we felt it was too hard to talk about. He was so young when he passed, but he was the best brother I could ever ask for. All he wanted was for everyone around him to be happy." Carmen stared off into the distance. "He was a comedian. Always laughing and making everyone else laugh right along with him. And handsome, oh my God. He drove all the girls around here crazy, but all he wanted to do was be with Laquita. Those two were like peas in a pod. I miss him so much," Carmen said, crying now. "He would've loved you."

Kameka stared at her aunt and placed a hand on her shoulder. "It's a'ight, Aunt Carmen."

"I'm sorry, Kameka."

"Sorry for what?"

"Everything. We should've been in your life. All of us." Carmen wiped her eyes with a tissue and blew her nose. "There might be some times when you hate me, but I'm going to do right by you. Antoine wouldn't have had it any other way."

"I'm not going to hate you, Aunt Carmen."

"I wouldn't speak so fast, but just know that everything I do is to make Kameka Dupree the best young lady she can possibly be," Carmen said, forcing a smile. "Now, where do you want to eat?"

"It doesn't matter," Kameka said, hunching her shoulders.

"Do you like Italian?"

"Nope."

"Ma'am."

"Nope, ma'am." Kameka smiled.

"Well, there's this little spot in Buckhead called Maggiano's. They have these stuffed mushrooms that are to die for. And their spinach dip is absolutely scrumptious."

"Sounds bougie, Aunt Carmen, but I'm wit it."

Carmen smiled and drove toward Buckhead.

Kameka turned in her seat and looked directly at Carmen. She didn't blink.

"What?" Carmen said.

Kameka continued her stare.

"Kameka, honey, is there something on your mind?"

"Bruce tried to have sex with me this weekend and when I told my mom, she said I was trying to take her man. Said I was fast, called me a little whore. That's why I'm coming to live with you. It's not about what Kevin did. I heard her telling you that lie. It's about me. She thinks I want her man."

Carmen sighed and looked at Kameka's shapely legs and thought about her being in the house with Sterling. Then she snapped the thought from her head and immediately felt guilty for even allowing it to go there in the first place.

The little girl's eyes cried out as she tried to hold on to her innocence, but her environment—a deceased father and an ill-prepared mother— was forcing her to grow up too quickly. Carmen was at a loss for words so she said the first thing that came to mind.

"I'm sorry to hear that, Kameka, but all that is behind you now. Let's leave the past in the past."

Kameka narrowed her eyes at her aunt and turned away. Carmen could tell that wasn't the answer she was expecting. Maybe she had already started letting Kameka down.

STERLING RUBBED his sweaty hands on his pants as he paced the floor. The last time he was this nervous he was hanging from the balcony on the sixteenth floor of a hotel in Miami. He didn't like the feeling then and he didn't like it now.

He cursed his luck. Just when things were going well in his life, he lost his job. He couldn't bring himself to tell Carmen, especially with them just getting married, that she would be responsible for all of the bills. Every time he attempted to tell her, he heard his father's words: *You gots to pay the cost to be the boss.*

The telephone rang and he stopped pacing and stared at it. After three rings he picked up the receiver and placed it to his ear without speaking.

"Hello," the voice said. "Is anyone there?"

"Hello," Sterling eased out.

"I'm calling for Sterling LaCour. Is this him?"

"Who's calling?"

"My name is Samantha Wells and I'm calling from Citibank. Mr. LaCour, your account is two months past due. When will you be mailing in a payment?"

Sterling breathed a sigh of relief. He had never been so happy to hear the voice of a bill collector in all of his life.

"Umm . . . well, I don't know when I'll be making a payment, but thanks for calling," Sterling said before hanging up on the young lady.

Less than a minute later the phone rang again. Sterling lifted it on the first ring and barked, "Listen lady from Citibank. Didn't I just tell you I didn't know when I'll have the money for that damn credit card? Do you think I figured that out since the last time you called me, two minutes ago? Stop harassing me." Sterling was about to hang up when he heard a familiar male voice.

"Good morning, Sterling."

A paralyzing fear overcame him. He was back on that balcony and he knew it would take a lot more than raising his voice to get this guy to go away. Why did he ever reopen this door to a past he'd love to forget? He asked himself over and over but he knew the answer. *You gots to pay the cost to be the boss.*

"L-L-Lincoln," Sterling stammered, trying to sound calm. "How's it going?"

"Well, my days are fine when I get paid, but when I don't they tend to be a little dark and dreary. So, Sterling, how *is* my day?" Lincoln asked calmly.

"I'll know in about an hour," Sterling replied nervously. "I'm waiting to hear from my accountant."

"Um-huh. I see. Accountant, huh?" Lincoln said, letting Sterling know his lie was not working.

"It's my wife's accountant, but I'm working something out to get you your twenty grand. We have to move a few assets around but we should be okay," Sterling said, trying to act as if twenty thousand dollars was no big deal.

There was nothing but silence on the other end of the phone. Not a good sign.

"If you can give me until tomorrow I should have your money."

A hand or something covered the mouthpiece of the phone, and Sterling couldn't make out the muffled conversation on the other end.

"Okay, Sterling, I understand life's little inconveniences so I'm going to give you a break. Twenty-four hours. Only now you owe me twenty-two grand."

"That's two grand for a one-day extension," Sterling said. "Kind of steep, don't you think?"

"Gambling's costly. If you would've won, I would've paid you, no problem. When you lose, I expect payment. You know my terms, two grand a day, and a week max. Just remember, time flies. And let me give you a word of advice. Don't gamble if you can't afford to lose," Lincoln said before hanging up.

"Damn you, Sam Cassell! You should've passed the ball to Sprewell or somebody. Troy Hudson was open right over in the corner," Sterling said, pointing to the corner as if he were talking to Sam Cassell himself. "And damn you, Flip Saunders, for drawing that fucked-up play. And damn you, Kevin Garnett, for being from South Carolina. Damn the whole Timberwolves organization for making me lose my money."

After letting out a stress-relieving yell, he calmed himself down and picked up the phone. Although he hated to let the cat out of the bag about his gambling—God knew they'd had their share of headaches when it came to him—he had to dial up his brother Jeff in South Carolina.

"Jeff, I need some money, like yesterday," Sterling said frantically.

"I guess I don't need to ask how you're doing," Jeff said as if he were just waking up.

"I'm in a little bind."

"Oh yeah, what's up?"

"Twenty grand," Sterling said in almost a whisper.

"What?"

"Twenty grand," he said a little louder.

"That's what I thought you said. Sterling, tell me you're not gambling again."

"Nah, me and Carmen just hit a little rough spot. We got a few IRS issues and she has a lot of student loans."

"Twenty grand, though?"

"I know it's kind of steep but we'll get it back to you in about three months."

Silence again.

"Let me speak to Carmen."

"She's not here."

"Well, have her call me."

"Why? My word's not good enough for you?"

"Nope."

"Man . . ."

"Sterling, you're lying. You're gambling again."

Busted.

"Listen, man, it was a one-time thing and it won't happen again."

"Sterling, I don't have that kind of money just lying around, and if I did I wouldn't give it to you. You should've learned the last five or six times you got caught up with those loan sharks."

"Come on, Jeff, now is not the time for the sermons. Plus don't forget what I did for you. I gambled your ass back to prosperity."

"You gonna throw that up in my face?"

"Man, forget all that. I need the money. These cats don't play. They know where I live and I can't put Carmen in harm's way like that. I'm just getting my life back together and I got something good here with Carmen."

"You should've thought about—"

"Not now, Jeff. I just had a little relapse is all. I'm asking for your help, man. Can you help me or not?"

There was a long pause and Sterling knew he had the money.

"Okay."

Sterling wanted to leap through the telephone line and kiss his brother. He closed his eyes and promised God this would be the last time he gambled. For real! This time he was for real.

"Can you FedEx me a money order?"

"I can't get it to you until Friday."

"Friday? Today is Monday!"

"I know, but that's the best I can do and you need to know that this is cleaning me out."

"Is there any way you can borrow it from someone and pay them back on Friday?"

"No!" Jeff roared. "Who in the hell do you think you are, Sterling? I have a family, or did you forget? When you pull little stunts like this it affects everyone. Not just you! This money I'm sending you on *Friday,* took four years for us to save. Now I have to hide this from my wife and pray to God nothing happens to Jeffrey. I promise you, this is your last withdrawal. And I want it back."

"Jeff, you know I'm good for it."

"I should've let those loan sharks in Philly toss you in the river. Or maybe I should've let the ones from New Orleans put that bullet through your head. You're nothing but a damn hustler. I feel sorry for Carmen. She probably doesn't even know the real you."

Sterling could hear the pain and frustration in his brother's voice, but later for that. All he needed right now was for Jeff to send the money.

"I'll get you your money back, Jeff."

"You better."

Click.

Sterling hung up the phone, waited for a dial tone, then dialed Lincoln's number.

"Yes," Lincoln said.

"I just spoke with our guy at the bank and he said he could make it happen by Friday. Is it possible to give me a little slack until then?"

"Sterling, you're well aware of my terms. Take as long as you need, just have me all of my money by next Monday."

Sterling sighed.

"Relax, Sterling, I'm not like the other guys you've dealt with. I don't break bones or kill people. I'm a businessman and time is money with me. So Friday will put you at thirty grand. I'll see you then."

5

NEW TROUBLE

allas sat on the edge of his desk, proud of what he saw before him. Every one of his students was participating in the class assignment. No small feat considering that when school started three weeks ago, he couldn't even get most of them to come to class. But after visiting some of their homes, and threatening physical harm to a few, he earned their trust as the kids started to realize that he really did care. They started showing up in class. And right now they were making him proud of his decision to stay at Alonzo Crim High School.

It didn't take long for word to get around that there was this special teacher with a gift to reach the unreachable. Once word got out, various schools put on a full-court press to recruit him, but the same philosophy he had about not abandoning his neighborhood applied to his job as well. So he decided not to leave the students of Crim High, which, by any measurement, was the worst school in the entire city of Atlanta. Seeing his kids so engrossed in their work made him think back to when he approached the principal about adding a philosophy course to the school's curriculum.

"Philosophy? You can barely get them to read and write. Don't you think asking them to think is a bit much?" she said, much to Dallas's surprise. He couldn't believe this was the same woman who got on the intercom every morning and preached about how smart and gifted the kids were. But he appealed her decision all the way to the governor and the course was added.

"Word association time," he said, much to the delight of his class. They whooped and hollered like they were kindergarteners at recess.

"When I say the word 'police,' what does that make you think?"

"Crooked," one child said.

"Enemy," another said.

"Dirty," yet another added.

"Okay, why do you feel that way, Joseph?" Dallas addressed the last student who answered.

"Because they're always messing with somebody for no reason. And they be planting stuff on folks," Joseph said.

"Okay, I can go with that. Now, how would you fix the problem of dirty police?" Dallas asked.

"Fire all of 'em and hire some new ones. Make sure they're all Christians."

"Oh no, cuz they crooked too," another student blurted out. "You should see how much they charge to go to church."

Dallas laughed.

"Okay, police officers are not the bad guys. It's all about attitude and it's up to you to change the way you'd like to be treated. Remember, we teach people how to treat us. Next word. What comes to mind when I say the word 'nigga'?"

Every hand shot up and he called on Jonnea, a young lady who had been arrested over thirty times and placed in nine different foster homes in her short sixteen years on earth. But here she was acting like a normal tenth grader, and that was almost all Dallas's doing.

"D.J.'s daddy," she said, much to the amusement of the class.

"Jonnea, go and stand in the hallway until I come out there," Dallas said, narrowing his eyes at her.

"But I was just kidding," she whined.

"If you want to use this precious time to act ignorant then do it outside by yourself. How many times do I have to tell y'all that life is not a game? It's about choices, and since you chose to blurt out that ignorance, I chose to have you stand in the hallway. Bye.

"Now, is there anyone else who wants to answer the question?" he asked. A few hands shot up. He called on a shy girl named Michelle, who used to dumb herself down so that she could fit in. Dallas had changed that too.

"I think of a black man," she said.

"Black man? That's an oxymoron," said Keith, the only Caucasian guy in the class. Keith was sent to Crim High by a juvenile judge after he was convicted of a hate crime. Keith and his skinhead friends got caught spray painting racial slurs on the house of some of their African-American neighbors.

"Mr. Dupree, you gonna let that baldhead Klansman sit up here and talk like that?" D.J. asked. "You made Jonnea go outside."

"We can work with this. Now, it's Keith's opinion that a black man doesn't exist. Anyone care to prove him wrong?"

"Well, I'm getting a little tired of the racist and I'mma show him after school what a black man can do when he feels disrespected," D.J. said.

"Show him what? That you can fight? Unless you plan on becoming a professional boxer, that little skill won't get you far in life. Besides, what will that prove?"

D.J. looked at Dallas as if he were crazy.

Dallas pointed to his head. "Use this. Now, I want you to find something between your two ears to use as a rebuttal. And never mind the fact that you're pissed. Control yourself and be constructive," he said with a calming smile. "Come on, D.J., brothers all over the world are counting on you," Dallas said with a smile.

D.J. shook his head. "Okay, first of all, the black man is God."

"Here we go with that crap," Keith said, throwing his hands up in a dismissive gesture.

"Even the Bible says it in plain English: Jesus had hair of wool, skin of bronze. If you ask me, that resembles my folks a whole lot more than it does yours. But never mind that. I got a million other examples of what a real black man is. You can thank the black man for getting you to school today in one piece because if it wasn't for a black man named Garrett Morgan and his traffic light, you and your overweight daddy wouldn't have made it here in that raggedy-ass car."

"At least I know my daddy," Keith responded.

"I know my daddy too, punk," D.J. said, getting out of his chair.

"Yeah, did you go and visit him this weekend at the big house?" Keith said, rolling his eyes but staying in his seat.

"Okay, you two. D.J., you were doing fine until you let your emotions take over. Sit down. You know Keith can't fight," Dallas said, causing laughter from the whole class, including Keith.

"Keith, you need to learn how to keep your stereotypical comments to yourself until you learn to do away with them altogether. Both of you get down and give me fifty push-ups," Dallas said, which was his preferred method of discipline for his guys. The girls, who could get just as rowdy as his boys, had to stand against the wall with their arms outstretched. Everyone except Jonnea, who was overweight and flat-out refused to do anything physical. He stood and let Jonnea back in.

The bell rang and the students started gathering their things. This was Dallas's last class for the day and he was happy for it because he couldn't wait to see his daughter. He would go to see Mrs. Locus tomorrow.

"Okay, guys, remember, tomorrow is test day. Keith, D.J., and Jonnea, sit tight for a minute."

Dallas stood and ushered his class out of the room. Once everyone was gone, he closed the door.

"Jonnea, what do you want to be when you grow up?"

"A hairdresser," she said tentatively, raising her eyes shyly.

"Jonnea, who gonna let you put your dirty hands on their heads?" D.J. said.

"D.J., shut up," Dallas barked.

"What is another word for hairdresser?"

"I don't know." Jonnea frowned.

"Well, you have twenty-four hours to figure it out. I need a five-page essay on why you want to become a hairdresser. Good-bye. I love ya," Dallas said.

Before she left, Jonnea offered a little smile, shot D.J. an evil look, and grabbed her book bag.

Dallas walked behind his desk, took a seat, and motioned for Keith and D.J. to sit down. He was determined not to give up on these two.

"Keith, what am I going to do with you?"

"Just let me do my time, Mr. Dupree."

"Why do you consider going to school doing time? You've been to jail; this is nothing like that."

"Worse."

"Now, how did you come up with that?"

"Mr. Dupree, I hope you don't take offense to this but I'd rather be around my own people."

"That's fair, and it's only natural for you to want to gravitate to what's comfortable to you. But you've proven over and over again you can't handle that. I want you to read this," Dallas said, handing Keith a paperback copy of *The Autobiography of Malcolm X.* "You have a week to complete it and write me a ten-page typed book report. You're a smart kid, Keith, but I'm afraid your hate is getting in the way of you realizing your full potential. Good-bye. Love ya."

"My dad is not going to let me bring this book in our house."

"If he has a problem with your school assignment, tell him to come see me."

"Can I have a pass for my next class?"

"Nope. If you didn't make me keep you late you wouldn't need a pass. See ya.

"D.J., how many times do I have to tell you to control yourself? You're just as bad as Keith. And what did I say about shooting down other people's dreams?"

D.J. smiled. "Mr. Dupree, I just be trippin', that's all."

"Well, stop trippin' and get serious. You are probably the smartest kid in this school but you act like a damn clown. Cut that out and handle your business. You set the tone for this whole class. So help a brother out, will ya?"

"A'ight, Mr. Dupree," D.J. said, throwing his book bag over his shoulder and easing out. Before he got to the door Dallas called his name.

"I need a ten-page essay on what it means to be a leader. Peace and love, black man."

Just as D.J. walked out, Kenya walked in.

"What's up, Mr. Dupree?"

"What's going on? I thought you had a class," Dallas said, throwing the last of his papers in his bag.

"I do, but I wanted to talk to you for a minute. You've been avoiding me all day. I didn't see you at lunch or in the break room."

"Been a little busy," Dallas said flatly. He wished she would go away.

"So it's like that?"

"Like what?"

"You screw me and then ignore me. If you just wanted the sex you could've said that."

"Why didn't you tell me you had a kid?"

"You didn't ask," Kenya said defensively. "Besides, what difference does it make?"

"I think it's disrespectful to have me up in your mother's house sexing you while your child and your mother are in the next room."

"Oh, see, you trippin'. I'm grown and that's my house. My mother lives with me, not the other way around, and my kids don't dictate what I do or who I do it with."

Kids? She has more? Dallas thought, but he kept his mouth closed.

"That's too bad. He seems to be a good kid. You should show him a little more respect."

"And you should mind your business and stop trying to save the world. You don't have all the answers. You might think you do but you're wrong!" Kenya shouted. "You ain't shit. And you need to know, I don't take too kindly to being used."

"You know what? Going out with you was a mistake. I should've gotten to know you a little better and maybe we wouldn't be having this conversation."

Kenya shook her head as if she had plans for Dallas.

Just then, the school's antiquated paging system clicked to life and the final announcements for the day were made. Taking advantage of the interruption, Dallas stood up and prepared to leave.

"I gotta go," Dallas said, walking out. He glanced back at Kenya, who angrily glared back.

"You'll pay for this, Mr. Dupree," Kenya said.

6

CULTURE SHOCK

*C*armen pulled up to Maggiano's on Peachtree Street in the heart of Buckhead and gave her keys to the valet.

"You just gonna leave the keys to your Benz with him?" Kameka asked with raised brows. "You don't even know him."

"Sure, he works here, honey. His job is to park the cars."

"Yeah, but my friends Bingo and Turk use to steal people's cars like that."

"You need to find some new friends," Carmen said, shaking her head as she got out of the vehicle.

Carmen walked up to the hostess and requested a nonsmoking table for two with a view. While they waited Carmen noticed a lady staring at Kameka with a contemptuous snarl. Carmen had to admit she was a little embarrassed by her niece's appearance and had considered whether she should bring her to such a nice establishment in her current attire—tight jeans, a revealing halter-top, and a ghetto fabulous hairdo—but she figured she had plenty of time to work on Kameka's appearance.

The lady then shifted her gaze to Carmen as if to say, *You should be ashamed to bring your child out of the house looking so uncouth.* Then a vague hint of recognition registered on her face. She walked over to them.

"Dr. LaCour?" the lady said.

"Yes?" Carmen said cautiously.

"Yancy Wingate from Jack & Jill. You spoke to our group of young ladies a few weeks ago," the lady in the sharp suit and expensive perfume said.

"Oh, yes," Carmen said, extending her hand to the lady, whom she really didn't remember. "How are you?"

"Marvelous. It's so good to see you again."

"Likewise. This is my niece Kameka."

"Nice to meet you, Kameka," Yancy said with a quick nod in Kameka's direction. She reached out and gave Kameka a limp handshake before quickly pulling her hand back.

Kameka picked up on the slight and rolled her eyes.

And she said I needed new friends, Kameka thought.

"A few of the young ladies were so motivated by your presentation they asked if I could arrange a hospital visit. If that's possible, I'd like to speak with you soon."

"Oh, I'd love that," Carmen said. "Maybe I can get my niece here involved with your organization."

Yancy scanned Kameka from head to toe, giving Carmen a weak smile. "It was nice seeing you again, Dr. LaCour. Let's talk," she said, handing Carmen a business card before walking away.

"Kameka, have you ever heard of Jack & Jill?"

"Nope," Kameka said, looking away.

"It's a social organization with some wonderful—"

"Aunt Carmen," Kameka interrupted, folding her arms, "I'm not interested. Especially if she has anything to do with it," Kameka said, staring at Yancy's back as she pranced away.

"She's the director of the organization and she's very connected. One thing you need to realize is that in this life it's all about who you know. I didn't care too much for her snobbish attitude either, but we may need her."

"I don't wanna know her."

Carmen didn't press the issue. They were called for their table and she motioned for Kameka to follow. She took a few steps toward the dining area before she noticed Kameka wasn't with her.

"Kameka," Carmen said as she stopped and looked back at her niece, who looked to be on the verge of tears.

Carmen walked back over to her.

"What's wrong, sweetie?" she said, placing a hand on her shoulder.

"I don't wanna eat here," Kameka said, crossing, then uncrossing her arms.

"Kameka, this is a really nice place. Just give it a try."

Kameka didn't move. She just stood there stiff as a board.

"Okay, let's go." Carmen sighed, giving up.

This teenage thing wasn't going to be easy, she thought.

Back in the car Carmen decided to let Kameka have her peace. The twenty-minute drive to her home was in complete silence. When they pulled up to her house, Sterling was in the driveway washing his 1964 Chevrolet Corvette.

"We're home," Carmen said, turning to Kameka. "Sweetie, I know this is an adjustment for you but we're going to be fine."

Kameka nodded.

Sterling ran over and opened Kameka's door. "Hey there, young lady. I haven't seen you in a while."

"Hi, Uncle Sterling," Kameka said dryly before walking toward the house.

"What's wrong with her?" Sterling asked Carmen as he removed Kameka's suitcase.

"I have no idea. I imagine she's a little homesick," Carmen said, watching Kameka walk into the house.

"You sure you're ready for this, Carmen?"

Carmen hunched her shoulders and sighed. "I don't have a choice."

Uncertainty was written all over Carmen's face.

"I'm going to need your support on this, Sterling. She's family and she's been through a lot with her mom and all," Carmen said, lifting her head and looking into her husband's doubtful eyes.

"I'm with you," Sterling said, taking Carmen into his arms.

Kameka entered the house that she'd visited only twice in her entire life, once when she'd turned thirteen and again when her uncle Dallas dropped by on their way to Six Flags amusement park. She looked around the lavish surroundings and felt uneasy. She wanted to go home. She looked around for a telephone and noticed the only sign of her being a part of this family: a framed picture of her taken when she was about ten years old. Kameka picked up the phone and dialed her mother's number. Bruce answered.

"Who dis?"

His voice brought back memories of him trying to ease himself under her sheets. Kameka held the phone to her ear, hoping he would just give the phone to her mother, but she realized that even if he did, she wasn't wanted there. She hung up the phone and tried to figure out her next move.

Kameka didn't really know her aunt Carmen or either of her uncles, and as far as she was concerned she wasn't family. She was just a throwback, the illegitimate offspring of their dead brother. When that reality set in, she had never felt so alone.

CARMEN WALKED in followed by Sterling, who was carrying Kameka's things.

"Kameka, you got a minute?"

Kameka nodded.

"I'm trying to figure out what I did wrong and I keep drawing blanks. You want to help an old lady out?"

Kameka stopped popping her chewing gum and looked at Carmen. It seemed as if all of her problems were on the tip of her tongue, but then she changed her mind about sharing them. It wouldn't do any good. "It's all good, Aunt Carmen. I'm just trippin'. Don't pay me no mind."

Carmen knew when she was being blown off. She decided to let it go for now. "Well, if you need to talk about anything, let me know," Carmen said, turning to walk into the kitchen.

"Why?" Kameka said. She tried to bite her tongue but that had never been her way.

"Excuse me?" Carmen said.

"Why would I come to you? You ain't gonna do nothing but say 'that's the past.' It's like if it ain't in your world then it don't matter," Kameka said, waving her hands around the large room before going back to popping her gum.

"That's not true," Carmen said, shaking her head and walking back over to her niece. "I care about whatever's going on with you."

"Oh yeah? What did I tell you when you first picked me up?"

Carmen frantically searched every nook and crevice of her mind for the correct answer but came up with nothing.

Kameka nodded knowingly and smiled. "Like I said, Aunt Carmen, it's all good. Where did you say I would be sleeping?"

Carmen looked down and her hands were shaking. She wanted to do right by her niece but had to question herself as to whether or not she had what it took.

"Kameka, listen, this is new to everyone. We all have to make adjustments and all I can tell you is, I'm going to give this my all."

"Sounds good. Where is that room, Aunt Carmen?"

Carmen sighed. "It's upstairs on the right," she said softly.

As Kameka climbed the stairs, Carmen's eyes followed her. Then Carmen raised her eyes a little higher.

"God, please guide me through this."

7

YOU GOT IT WRONG

*A*s Dallas pulled up to the modest single-family ranch-style home in College Park, a suburb on the outskirts of Atlanta, he felt a surge of happiness as he always did when he reunited with his daughter after her visits with Yasmin's family. He jumped out of his truck and headed toward the house.

"Da-ddyyyyyy," Aja screamed as she ran down the wooden porch steps.

Dallas dropped down to one knee and opened his arms to make way for his little bundle of joy, who today looked more like a boy. Gone were the long silky locks that her mother wanted her to have.

"Hey there, pretty girl. How ya doing?" he said, looking curiously at her new hairstyle.

"Fine," she said, burying her face in her daddy's broad chest and wrapping her arms around his neck.

"Now, you know that don't make no sense," Mrs. Gibson said, standing on the porch and shaking her head. "You would think y'all haven't seen each other in years."

"What happened to your hair?" Dallas asked, fingering the mini Afro.

"I had to cut it," Mrs. Gibson said. "She got some candy stuck in it."

Dallas took a big breath. He had for a while been worrying about leaving his daughter alone with her aging grandparents. Mr. Gibson was confined to a wheelchair and hadn't uttered a word in over six months. Mrs. Gibson appeared to be in good health, but she had been acting a little weird lately. He figured no amount of fussing was going to bring his baby's beautiful hair back so he let it go.

"A'ight, Aja, run and get your things," Dallas said, standing up. Aja ran into the house.

"Did you see Elvis playing cards with Martin Luther King this morning?" Mrs. Gibson asked.

"Where?" Dallas asked, confused. He was sure she was talking about a television show.

"They were right out here! I'll tell you, Elvis can't play a lick of pity pat," she said, laughing.

That was it. Dallas smiled and made a mental note never to let his daughter stay another night alone with the woman who had obviously started her descent into senility.

Aja ran back outside with her little pink-and-white suitcase.

"Give your grandmother a hug. We gotta run," Dallas said.

Aja did and they said their good-byes and headed home.

AS DALLAS turned onto his street he saw a throng of men, women, and children carrying bats, chains, and various other weapons. Baldhead appeared to be their leader. Dallas pulled into his driveway and Baldhead rushed over to look in the backseat of Dallas's truck. When he saw Aja, he looked relieved. Dallas parked in front of his garage.

"What's up, Baldhead?" he said, getting out of the truck and motioning toward the crowd.

"Man, you heard the news?" Baldhead said, running to the rear of the passenger side to open Aja's door. "They got a plum fool running 'round here messing with babies. Done took Mrs. Mack's daughter and violated her something terrible. They said he got another one too. I was praying it wasn't little Aja. Lord knows that fool would have hell to pay if he touched this little girl," he said, unbuckling Aja's seatbelt.

"I heard it on the radio on the way over here," Dallas said, shaking his head.

"Li'l Nikki wasn't nuttin but seven years old, man," Baldhead said, near tears. "I swear to Gawd, if I catch that sum bitch—scuse me, Aja," Baldhead said, covering his mouth before any more foulness slipped out. "He'll be pushin' up daisies. Sure as my name is Mario Jackson."

"Daddy, what happened?" Aja asked.

"There's a bad man running around here, baby."

Baldhead turned away, clearly shaken up by today's turn of events. "Man, it don't make no sense. Kids should be off-limits."

"Where is Mrs. Mack right now?"

"I guess she down at Grady Hospital with Nikki," Baldhead said. "I gotta go, Dallas. We gonna catch this fool. Just keep little Aja close by."

"Baldhead," Dallas called out as Baldhead started out of the driveway. "Be careful, and I appreciate you looking out, brah."

"You know how we do."

Just as Baldhead cleared the yard a police cruiser eased into Dallas's driveway and stopped behind his truck. The pack of people stopped, hoping to hear whatever news the officers had about the molester.

Two plainclothes detectives got out of the cruiser. The black officer, whom Dallas knew from Priest's days in the department, got out of the passenger side. He too looked like the day's events had shaken him. The driver, a white officer with a buzz cut who looked to be fresh out of the academy, jumped out of the vehicle with his hand a little too close to his gun.

"How's it going, Sergeant Lewis?" Dallas said, taking a quick glance at Mr. Buzz Cut.

"How you doing, Dallas? You got a minute?" Sergeant Lewis asked.

"Sure."

"Do you have anyone to watch your little girl while we talk?"

"Sure. I can run her across the street to Mrs. Morton's house."

"Why don't you do that," Officer Lewis said in an uneasy tone.

"I'll be right back," Dallas said as he lifted his girl up and headed across the street. Two minutes later he was back.

"What's up?"

Officer Lewis sighed and had trouble getting the words out.

"Dallas, we have a little problem."

"I heard about it. What can I do to help?"

"It's not what you think," Officer Lewis said, shaking his head. "There was a complaint made against you."

That damn Kenya, Dallas thought.

"What kind of complaint?"

"Dallas, first let me tell you, I don't believe this for one minute but I have a job to do."

"What kind of complaint are you talking about, Sarge?"

Officer Lewis sighed and it seemed like forever before he spoke again.

"Aggravated assault and rape."

Dallas closed his eyes and quickly shook his head. Did he hear Sergeant Lewis correctly? He couldn't have heard him correctly.

"Excuse me?" He felt like his world was crumbling.

"Yeah, I was shocked too, but what can I say?"

"Turn around and place your hands behind your back," Mr. Buzz Cut barked.

"Is this some kind of joke? Is Priest behind this?"

"Turn around and place your hands behind your back. Now. I'm not asking again." Buzz Cut's command was loud enough for the pack of people to hear. He removed his handcuffs and took a few steps toward Dallas.

"Hey," Lewis said to his partner. "Calm down. I've known this boy since he was ten years old. Now, you let me handle this."

Dallas's heart rate increased to a million beats per second and he couldn't stop his hands from shaking. No, this was not his brother's way of getting him to talk. This was real.

"You guys have the wrong man. This has to be some kind of mistake," Dallas said.

"There is no mistake. The victim has signed a sworn statement and she's undergone a medical examination," Mr. Buzz Cut said arrogantly. "You're under arrest. You have the right to remain silent—"

Mrs. Morton walked up the driveway holding Aja.

"Wait a minute," Lewis said to his partner, halting the Miranda rights.

"Do you want to take this opportunity to ask them to leave?" Buzz Cut said, pointing to Mrs. Morton and Aja.

Dallas's mind froze. He stared into his daughter's innocent eyes. How could this happen? All of his life, he'd made a conscious effort to avoid trouble, and although he knew this was some kind of mistake, it didn't make him feel any better.

"Daddy," Aja said, reaching out for him. "I want my daddy."

He wanted to take his daughter in his arms and tell these guys in suits to kiss his behind, but that would only make things worse. For the first time in his life, he couldn't be there for his daughter. He never wanted to feel this way again.

Aja was only three years old, but she was a very bright three-year-old. She could read, write, and do some arithmetic, and the tears in her eyes said she was adding this up to be a horrible situation for her father. All he could do was pray Mr. Buzz Cut wouldn't place the handcuffs on him in front of her.

"Mrs. Morton, will you take Aja in your house? And call Carmen; I have to ride somewhere with these guys."

"Daddy, what's wrong?" Aja said, fighting to get out of Mrs. Morton's arms. "I want you, Daddy."

"Mrs. Morton, please take Aja in your house," Dallas pleaded, almost on the verge of tears himself. "Baby, I'll be home soon. It's okay. I promise," he said, hoping and praying that his words would hold true.

Mrs. Morton hurried back home without any questions. She had heard that note of urgency in too many black men's voices and knew exactly what it meant—trouble.

Aja cried out for Dallas and the sound was pure torture to his ears.

"I want my Daddy," Aja cried as she pounded her little hands on Mrs. Morton's shoulders. "Daddy. Daddy."

Baldhead, who had stood on the corner watching the whole turn of events, walked up in the yard when he saw Dallas with his hands on the hood of the police car.

"Man, why y'all ain't out there looking for that rapist?" he demanded of the officers. "Dallas a teacher."

"Sir, will you please step back?" Buzz Cut said.

"No, I cannot step back. What's the problem, white bread?"

"Sir, at this point you're interfering with a police investigation and therefore obstructing justice."

"Kiss my ass. I'll holla and have this whole mob act a fool."

Buzz Cut stiffened up. He looked at the angry crowd edging their way into the yard and fumbled with the radio on his shoulder.

"Twenty-two seventy-three requesting backup at nine Willow Street."

"How you gonna call for backup just because I want some answers?"

"Sir, you look like you're under the influence of narcotics."

"And you look like you need to take a shit," Baldhead growled. "But I ain't called no doctor to give you no enema."

"Officer Glaze, cancel that request for backup. Mario, why don't you go on home?" Officer Lewis urged calmly. "Now, you folks go on home. Dallas will be all right."

"Nah, Lewis. I need to know what the problem is. They got a damn rapist running around here and y'all numb nuts trynna lock up the one of the few good brothers we got," Baldhead yelled at the cops.

"Baldhead, calm down. This is just some kind of mistake. I'll be all right," Dallas said, still having trouble believing his own words.

"Nah, Dallas. All them computers they got, they shouldn't be making no mistakes," Baldhead said, staring at the police officers, daring them to move. "I got five warrants and ain't nobody come looking for me."

"Oh, yeah?" Buzz Cut said, removing his pistol from its holster and pointing it at Baldhead. "Then, turn around and place your hands behind your back."

Dallas shook his head. He couldn't believe Baldhead could be so stupid.

Baldhead, who wasn't fazed by Buzz Cut's gun, calmly walked over to stand beside Dallas and placed his hands on the hood of the car.

"What're you doing?" Dallas asked.

"Looking out for you," Baldhead replied as he stared straight ahead. "Just looking out for you, li'l brah."

8

HAVE YOU SEEN HER?

"*G*et your filthy hands off of me!" the old man screamed at Carmen as she attempted to check his vital signs. "I want a man doctor."

Carmen removed her hand from the arm of the old man with old ways who came in to the emergency room frequently thinking the world should stop because he had a headache, and calmly walked out of the examination room. As a young black female doctor in a predominantly white hospital, she had become immune to the insults and lack of confidence in her abilities.

"Call Dr. Wilcox," she told the nurse who was standing by. "I'm taking a break."

Carmen was heading toward the physician's lounge for a much-needed break when her pager went off. She looked down at the screen; it read FULTON COUNTY.

"Dr. LaCour," Carmen said, returning the page.

"Carmen, this is Joanne," her friend whispered. "We have a little problem."

Joanne Fox was Carmen's friend from undergraduate school. She also worked as a counselor at the private high school where Kameka was now registered.

Carmen closed her eyes and shook her head. *Not on her first day,* she thought.

"I'm listening."

"Your niece was in a fight, and she beat the girl up pretty bad. Her parents are here and they're talking about filing assault charges against Kameka."

"You're kidding!"

"I wish I was."

"Oh my God," Carmen said, squeezing her eyes shut, willing away the pounding that was building in her head. "What happened?"

"I don't really know," Joanne said. "But I can tell you the young lady who was on the receiving end is one of those 'privileged' ones whose daddy has a gazillion dollars, and believe you me, she acts the part."

Carmen took a deep breath and removed her stethoscope and jacket. "I'm on my way."

As Carmen drove over to the high school a million thoughts ran through her head. Was she doing the right thing by allowing Kameka to come and live with her? Maybe Kameka was too old to change. She read once that a child's personality was fully developed by the time he or she was ten years old. Kameka was sixteen. Maybe it was too late. Could Kameka shed her ghetto mentality? Carmen wondered if she had the patience to deal with a teenager. *Damn Laquita and everyone like her,* Carmen thought. How dare they have children knowing they are unprepared to raise them properly! For people like Laquita, kids were just a product of a freaky night.

Carmen pulled into the school parking lot and gripped the steering wheel as she took a couple of deep breaths to calm herself. She entered the building, which looked more like an office complex than a high school. The message was clear; Cambridge Academy was all about business.

"Hello, my name is Carmen LaCour," she said to the receptionist, who offered a warm smile. "I'm here to see Dr. Preside."

"Is he expecting you?"

"No, but my niece had a little incident today, and I would like to speak with him."

"What is your niece's name?"

"Kameka Jenkins."

The lady's smile disappeared and was replaced by a look of disgust. Then she caught herself and gave Carmen a forced smile.

"Follow me, please," she said.

The receptionist led Carmen into the oversized office of the school's director. Behind his desk were pictures of him shaking hands with former statesmen George Bush, Sr., Bill Clinton, and Al Gore, and a larger photo of him riding in a golf cart with Michael Jordan. Other photos included Jay Leno, and there was one of Atlanta Falcons owner, Arthur Blank, handing him a check at a fund-raiser.

"Good morning, Dr. LaCour." Dr. Preside rose to shake her hand.

Dr. Preside was a pleasant-looking man who appeared to be in his late fifties, maybe early sixties, although it was evident he was a client of the Hair Club for Men.

Why can't white men just let it go? Bald is in, Carmen thought.

"Thank you for coming. Please have a seat. This is Mary and Robert Doyle and their daughter, Catherine."

"Where is Kameka?"

"She's in with Mrs. Fox, the school's counselor."

Carmen waited for them to get up and shake her hand, but it didn't look like it was going to happen so she sat across from the Doyles. She glanced at Catherine and it was pretty clear that she had officially received her first ghetto ass whipping. She wore a funky pair of Jackie Onassis shades but Carmen could still see the discoloration around both eyes.

"Dr. LaCour, there was a misunderstanding today and we—" Dr. Preside began.

"There was no misunderstanding," Catherine snapped. "Everyone knows that I'm not to be disturbed when I'm eating my lunch. Your daughter or whoever she is has to be taught some respect."

"Catherine, I was talking. Now if you want respect you have to give it in return," Dr. Preside said calmly. But he was clearly getting frustrated with the young lady.

"Don't you dare talk to my daughter in that manner," Mrs. Doyle said. "She's already been through enough today without you adding to it."

Mr. Doyle sat stoically, rubbing his hand through his beard.

"My apologies, Catherine, but as we all know, fighting of any kind is not tolerated here at Cambridge. To do so is grounds for immediate expulsion."

"Good, then it's settled," Catherine said, standing. "She's expelled."

"What happened?" Carmen asked Dr. Preside, ignoring Catherine. *This child isn't going to run me,* she thought.

"There's nothing left to talk about. If she leaves she doesn't go to jail," Catherine said in a manner that said she was used to giving orders.

Carmen kept her eyes on Dr. Preside.

"I'm waiting."

"Well, like I said, there was a little misunderstanding and—"

"I asked her twice to remove herself from my space and when she didn't obey, I slapped her. Then like some wild . . . animal she attacked me. That cannot happen. I'm all for helping out the blacks but not at the cost of my own safety," Catherine interrupted again.

"So, Dr. Preside, where do we go from here?" Carmen asked, smiling inside that Kameka had done what Catherine's parents had obviously failed to do.

He leaned back in his chair and seemed to be in deep thought before he spoke.

"Do you plan on keeping Kameka here?" he asked her.

Carmen couldn't believe what she had just heard.

"Do you plan on keeping Catherine here?"

"I'm asking because . . . well, I was hoping there was an amicable way we could resolve this issue without getting the authorities involved."

"From what you've told me, Kameka acted in self-defense. So, in my eyes, as well as the law's, she did nothing wrong."

"She attacked me and you don't see anything wrong with that?" Catherine spat, slamming herself back down in the chair.

"No," Carmen said, not really interested in having a conversation with the spoiled child.

"Listen." Mr. Doyle spoke for the first time. "We give a lot of money to this school, and if you'd like to continue receiving those checks I suggest you end this meeting right now and call the authorities. That child should be arrested."

"Why don't we do that?" Carmen said.

"I'm sure we can come to—" Dr. Preside stated again.

"Robert, you call the police," Mrs. Doyle commanded, and her husband quickly obeyed. He told the police his location and within five minutes two burly cops walked into the office.

Both of them walked over to Robert Doyle and shook his hand while smiling the whole time.

"I want the person who did this to my daughter arrested," Mrs. Doyle demanded as her daughter removed her sunglasses.

"Who did it?" one of the officers said, looking directly at Carmen.

"Her name is Kameka something or other," Catherine said.

One of the police officers reached for his handcuffs. That's when Carmen had had enough.

"So you're ready to arrest someone just because they asked you to? Have you ever heard of probable cause? Have you ever been sued? This young lady hit my niece, who had no other option but to defend herself. So if my niece is going to jail today, then I suggest you ask your partner to remove his handcuffs as well, because Catherine Doyle will be joining her."

The room became quiet. So quiet that you could hear a mouse pee on a cotton ball.

"Ma'am, do you see this young lady's face?" one of the officers said, motioning toward Catherine. "Now, unless your niece looks similar, she's going to jail." He turned to Dr. Preside. "Dr. Preside, where is this young lady?"

Suddenly it was clear to Carmen. She was in a room with these very powerful and rich white people, and the police were there to protect them first and uphold the law second. All of her life she had somehow managed to step above racism but today she wasn't in the mood, and the look in the policemen's eyes told her she was still a second-class citizen as far as they were concerned. She pulled out her cell phone and dialed.

"Hello, may I speak to Jackie?" Carmen stood and walked over to the officer who had threatened to take Kameka to jail and read his name tag. "This is Carmen LaCour and I have an Officer Vincent here who says he's taking my niece to jail." Carmen listened and then responded. "Well, she didn't initiate the incident. She was slapped and then she defended herself and . . . Yes. Sure, one moment." Carmen handed the phone to Officer Vincent.

"Ma'am, you can have your lawyer meet us down at the jail. I don't have anything to say to him or her," Officer Vincent said arrogantly.

"It's not my lawyer; I suggest you take this phone."

Officer Vincent hesitated before snatching the phone from Carmen's hand. He placed it close to his ear, making sure it didn't touch his skin.

"Officer Vincent," he snapped. As he listened he at first became pale, then redder and redder. "Yes, ma'am. No, ma'am. I . . . I . . . apologize. Okay. Yes, Chief. I understand. Thank you. Good-bye." Officer Vincent handed Carmen her phone nicely. "I'm sorry for the misunderstanding, Dr. LaCour. Dr. Preside, this is your issue. Whatever you decide is fine with us. You take care." Officer Vincent nodded at his partner and they hurried out of the office.

"Where are they going? I want her arrested. She hit me," Catherine whined. She was on the verge of tears as she watched the police officers leave.

"Catherine, you can't hit people and not expect them to hit back," Dr. Preside said. "Now, I'm going to give both you and Kameka a warning and put this matter to rest."

"Billy, you can kiss the endowment good-bye," Mrs. Doyle said, standing and fixing her dress.

Dr. Preside didn't respond.

"Catherine, collect your things, because you will not be attending this school anymore. And as for you," Mrs. Doyle said to Carmen, "you have not heard the last of me."

Carmen smiled and removed a business card. She held it out for her, but Mrs. Doyle ignored it.

Dr. Preside looked relieved as the Doyles walked out of his office.

Once the Doyles were gone, Carmen turned to Dr. Preside and hunched her shoulders. "I'm sorry you lost that check, but I have to protect my niece."

"I understand, but losing that check isn't so bad. They donated a lot of money but I think we'll be just fine without it. The Doyles are some first-class assholes," he said with a wide grin. "Please forgive me for speaking so frankly."

"No, I couldn't agree more."

"In thirty years of being an educator I've never run across a more spoiled child than Catherine Doyle. I knew the minute she walked in here that whatever the problem was, it more than likely originated with her."

"Well, I know how hard it is to do the right thing when large sums of money are involved, so please accept my heartfelt gratitude," Carmen said as she stood to leave.

"Well, I may not have this job for long, but that sure did feel good. I'm sure the board of directors won't view this decision as a sound one, but I felt it was the right thing to do," Dr. Preside said, shaking Carmen's hand. "After all, we're in the business of teaching and I don't think it sends the right message when we allow folks preferential treatment just because they have a nice-size checkbook."

"I couldn't agree more. Plus I would've sued you, and that could've been costly," Carmen said with a straight face.

"Please tell Kameka we have no issues. All is forgotten. But that the next time she has a problem with one of the students, there are other ways to solve it."

Carmen shook Dr. Preside's hand and left the office. She felt as if she had made a new friend.

"HAVE YOU seen Kameka?" Carmen asked Sterling as she rushed into the house, throwing her purse down on the sofa and heading for the stairs.

"Isn't she in school?"

"No, she was in a fight and left. Did she call?"

"A fight?" Sterling said to Carmen's back as she ran up the stairs. "Why was she fighting?"

Carmen came back down and grabbed her purse.

"You want me to ride with you?"

Carmen stopped and stared at Sterling, who wore slacks, dress shoes and a tank top. "What are you doing home from work so early?"

"I finished my project, so I decided to take the rest of the day off. I called you but you didn't answer. I was hoping to get a little spontaneous quality time," Sterling said, walking over to his wife and putting his arms around her waist. He kissed her neck.

"Oh," Carmen said, slipping away, "if I stay here, I'll never find my niece. Maybe tonight." She stood on tiptoe to kiss his lips.

Just as she reached for the telephone to call Laquita, it rang.

"Hello," Carmen said. "Oh, hi, Jeff."

Sterling's insides did somersaults.

"Sure," Carmen said with a frown aimed in Sterling's direction. "He's right here. Would you like to speak with him? Okay . . . will do. Thanks a lot." Carmen paused. Whatever Jeff said had altered her mood.

"Sterling, is there anything you want to tell me?"

Sterling smiled nervously. "Not that I know of. What's up?"

"Jeff said there was a little problem with the money and he couldn't get it to you until next week. Said to give him a call. Why are you borrowing money from your brother?"

"It's for some investments."

Carmen nodded, but she could tell by the tone of Jeff's voice that that call wasn't about any investments.

"Well, I have to find Kameka, so I'll see you a little later," Carmen said, grabbing her purse and walking out the door. She'd deal with Sterling later.

9

PRIESTLY DUTIES

*P*riest Dupree was a man of few words who stood an imposing six feet four inches tall. His sculptured muscles and long arms reminded many of a young Muhammad Ali. He wore his hair closely cropped and his almond-colored skin was as smooth as the day is long. His clothes were made from the finest fabrics; he drove a three-hundred-and-fifty-thousand-dollar Mercedes Maybach and lived on a ten-acre farm. Despite his outward trappings of success, he was unhappy with the world he lived in.

Priest snapped his head toward the fifty-inch plasma television hanging over the fireplace. A familiar face was on the screen. He narrowed his eyes at the picture of the man just above the right shoulder of the evening newscaster. Priest turned up the volume.

"Marvin Michaels, a high-level member of the Dreamland drug cartel, was found shot to death in the driveway of his southwest Atlanta home. Officials are saying it appears to be a turf war. A six-year-old girl was struck in the neck by a stray bullet. She is in critical condition at Fulton Memorial. Neighbors expressed outrage that something like this could happen in their backyards." Monica Kaufman, the newscaster, gave her report as the camera zoomed in on a rail-thin lady with pink rollers in her hair and about three teeth.

Five-hundred-thousand-dollar houses in that neighborhood and they find the one crackhead to interview, Priest thought.

"That li'l baby didn't do nothing to nobody and they come through here just a shootin'," the lady said. "The man upstairs gonna take care of them devils, I'll promise you that. The truth always finds its way to the light."

Priest twisted his neck to relieve tension. He heard his cell phone ring and before he could turn to get it, he heard Mina's pumps clicking against the marble floors, headed his way.

The product of a black father and a Vietnamese mother, Mina was beautiful in every sense of the word, but she was an outcast in her country. She had olive skin and silky black hair that flowed smoothly down her back. She was nearly six feet tall, mostly legs. But her external beauty was nearly overshadowed by her wonderful spirit. Being with Priest was the only thing that made her feel at home.

THEY MET three years ago on the same day Priest was fired from the Atlanta Police Department. He'd been pissed off, stressed out, and heartbroken over the loss of the only job he truly loved. Priest decided he'd take the advice of his lieutenant who had just given him his walking papers and go get an oriental massage.

Priest pulled his old Ford F-150 up to a cheesy massage parlor with a sign in pink neon lights in the shape of a woman. He walked into the dark little waiting room and took a seat. Three scantily clad women walked from behind a curtain but there was only one who caught his eye. He took the tall woman's hand and immediately changed his mind about the massage. All he could think about was how good it had to feel to get lost between those long creamy legs. He felt his manhood rise as she led him into a room with a bed and a chair. She asked him to undress and she began doing the same. Priest looked into her eyes as she disrobed and suddenly had a change of heart. Over the years he had seen too many women taken advantage of. Visions of his own mother flashed through his mind and the things he knew she had done for money once her addiction took hold of her. The woman lay on her back on the bed and opened her legs.

She moved as if she was programmed to perform sex. He took a seat in the chair and just stared at her. Her eyes never left the ceiling but Priest could see the pain. She waited for him to mount her and do what he supposed hundreds or maybe thousands of other men had done.

"What's your name?" he asked.

"Mina," she said, still looking up at the ceiling.

"It's nice to meet you, Mina. My name is Priest, and I'm not going to be having sex with you today."

She shot up quickly and turned in his direction. He showed her his badge, which only he knew no longer carried any weight. Her eyes grew large.

"I d-d-did no wrong?" she stammered fearfully in broken English.

"Who do you work for?"

"Please, let me make it up to you. I do anything you like," she said, vigorously shaking her head from side to side. "Just don't tell Lord."

Lord? Priest recalled the street moniker of a small-time pimp whom he'd arrested a few times, back when he was working vice.

"Lord Jamal?" Priest asked, hoping it was the same guy. Mina's eyes registered the fear that Lord Jamal's hand had brought to girls for as long as Priest could remember. He was what street folks would call a gorilla pimp. Even barely making it to five feet tall, he ruled his girls with fear. He carried out all kinds of atrocities, from coat-hanger beatings to straight-up mutilations.

"My Momma-san is to be alerted," Mina said, tears flowing freely down her face.

"Where is your Momma-san?"

"She's out front."

"What's her name?"

"Helen," Mina said softly. "I'll be disciplined, so will you please allow me to make whatever it is I did up to you?"

"Honey, you haven't done anything to me," Priest said, trying to calm the young lady. "How long have you been working here?"

"One week. My family owes money, and I don't want to dishonor them by trouble," Mina said.

"Get dressed," Priest said as he stood and walked out.

After a brief conversation with Helen, it took Priest less than an hour to find Lord Jamal. He was sitting at the bar of a hole-in-the-wall club, harassing the customers. When Priest entered, his eyes were immediately attracted to Jamal's lime green Versace knock-off shirt, orange pants, and wide brim hat with a purple feather. He looked like a damn fool. Priest walked over to the bar and snatched Jamal up by the back of his shirt.

"Hey, muthafucka, unass me," Jamal shouted, but he stopped when he saw the only man in the Atlanta Police Department that he feared. Priest was known to the street guys for not playing by department rules, so they tried their best to steer clear of him because they never knew what to expect.

Priest pushed him out the back door into the alley.

"We have a li'l problem, Jamal," Priest said, slamming him up against the brick wall.

"Dupree, why you sweatin' me? I ain't even in your jurisdiction no more," Jamal said, straightening out his clothes.

"You lied to me, and you know how I hate to be lied to."

"Man, whatchu jaw jacking 'bout?"

"You were supposed to leave the pimp game. I gave you a break and all you did was switch locations. Instead of the streets, you use massage parlors. Instead of young black girls, you use Asians. Why you trynna play me?"

"Come on, Dupree," Jamal whined in his high-pitched pimp's slang. "You know the game, baby. What else I'mma do?" He held his arms wide. "Baby, I'm a pimp. P.I.M.P. It's in my blood. My daddy was a pimp, and his daddy was a pimp. Hell, I did a little research and I found out I'm from a pimp tribe in Africa. For all I know my ancient granddaddy was the one who sold your black-ass people into slavery. Pimping in the motherland, baby."

Despite his disgust of the man, Priest smiled. Jamal was always good for a laugh, even if he was scum.

"Jamal, tomorrow at noon, I will meet you here and you will bring me every last girl you got out here selling ass."

Jamal folded his arms and looked away. Priest read the defiance and grabbed Jamal by the collar. He shoved the barrel of his .40-caliber Glock pistol as far down Jamal's throat as it would go. Jamal's eyes bugged out.

"What's the matter, Jamal, you not used to having something hard and black in your mouth? Not that pleasant of a taste, huh? Well if you don't have those girls here tomorrow, I promise you'll get used to it," Priest barked. "Tomorrow at noon. Right here."

The next day Jamal showed up with thirteen girls—nine Asian, two white, and two black.

"I can't find the others, man. They hiding out."

"You better not let me find out you still working, you little piece of shit," Priest said before loading the girls up and taking them to a friend's battered women's shelter. A few of the girls scoffed at the idea and they were allowed to leave, but most of them wanted to better themselves and took advantage of their opportunity. Mina was one of the ones who didn't go to the shelter. She moved in with Priest. It took her a few weeks to grasp that she wasn't sold off to another pimp. By the time she realized that she was free to come and go as she pleased, she didn't want to be anywhere else.

Mina opened up to Priest about how her family sent her to the United States to pay back a debt her stepfather owed for cattle. He used the cattle to earn enough money to send her two brothers to college.

MINA HANDED Priest the phone, turned around, and made her way back to the bedroom.

"Talk to me," he said.

"Priest, Dallas is in trouble," Carmen cried. "They arrested him."

"Whoa, calm down a second. What's going on?"

"They're holding him for rape. You know he wouldn't do anything like that!"

"Carmen, calm down. Where are you?"

"I'm at home. I was going to go to the jail downtown but they said they didn't set bail and weren't sure if they would."

"Okay, you stay put. I'll take care of it."

"Priest, we gotta get him out of there."

"I'm on it. Try to calm down."

Priest ended the call. With his elbows on his knees, he placed his face in his large hands and took a minute to plan his next move. He stood and walked over to a glass shelf that held the last picture his family ever took together. In the photo he was standing between his brother Antoine and Carmen, with his hands on his mother's shoulders. Dallas lay at her feet.

Priest stared at the little boy in the photo and remembered the night he became family.

IT WAS ALMOST three o'clock in the morning when Priest and Antoine snuck out of the house. The past few nights they had heard a howling sound. He had awakened his mother when he heard the sound, but she said it was a wild animal and to go back to sleep. But he couldn't sleep because whatever it was sounded like it was in pain.

Priest woke up Antoine and they decided to do a little investigating of their own.

They followed the noise to an old rundown house a hundred feet away from the projects they called home. They crept around the house, where they saw a flicker of candlelight. Easing up to the first-floor window, Priest peeked in. He saw what appeared to be a child tied to a pole. Antoine got down on his hands and knees while Priest stood on his back to get a better view, and what he saw changed him forever. It was a little boy, lying in his own feces, naked as a newborn. He reminded Priest of one of those commercials for Feed the Children. He looked scared, angry, and confused. Priest broke the window with his bare hands and climbed in. The smell was almost unbearable. He heard rats scurrying around on the floor near his feet. Antoine crawled through the window and stood beside his brother. The room was still kind of dark, so they eased their way over to the little boy and tried to lift him. He seemed so fragile and was so light, they thought he would snap under their grip.

They heard a noise. Someone was coming.

Priest put as much bass in his voice as he could when he said, "Atlanta Police Department. Don't move!"

He got exactly what he wanted. The next sound he heard was footsteps running off in the other direction. Lifting the little boy by his hands and feet, Priest and Antoine carried him home.

Exhausted, they laid the little one on their porch. Barely clinging to life, he spoke in a voice just above a whisper when he told them that his foster mother had tied him to a bed and forgotten about him. He said he didn't remember the last time he had eaten and that he was eight years old. He couldn't remember what his name was, but he did remember he was born in Dallas, Texas. Then he passed out. Priest held the little boy's head in his lap while Antoine ran into the house and woke their mother.

"What y'all boys done got into now?" Sara Dupree said, throwing on her housecoat. "Oh my God," she gasped, holding her hand over her mouth. She had never seen such a sight.

"Go in the house and call the ambulance. Lord, the baby got a rope around his neck," Sara said as she sat down on the porch and placed the little boy's head in her lap.

"Priest, go in and get a blanket to cover this baby up."

It wasn't until the paramedics arrived and removed the blanket that they noticed sores all over the little boy's skin.

Dallas spent six weeks in the hospital being fed by a tube and clinging to life by hope and a prayer. The doctors called his survival a miracle, but Priest knew differently. He could feel the sores on his knees from the hours he'd spent at night praying for the little boy's recovery. Sara allowed all of her kids to visit him daily as if he were her own son. She got the adoption paperwork started the minute she was told that once he was well he would be placed back in a different foster home. And once he recovered, the state didn't put up much of a fight when Sara came to pick him up. After all, his former foster parent had slithered away in the middle of the night like the snake she was.

PRIEST PUT the family photo back on the shelf.

"Mina, I'll be back shortly. I gotta go get my brother."

*D*allas sat in the back of the police car in total shock. How could this happen to him? Why was this happening to him? He knew in his heart that life threw obstacles your way just to keep you on your toes. God knows he'd had his share: homelessness, neglect, physical abuse, mental abuse, and all before the ripe old age of nine. But he couldn't figure this one out. Over and over his mind tried to churn out a reason, but to no avail.

THREE MONTHS after Yasmin had passed away, Dallas woke up to find his brother Priest standing over him.

Dallas jumped and tried to catch his breath.

"Man, what are you doing in my house?"

Priest didn't answer. He just smiled and walked over

to the window. He pulled the shades open and blinded Dallas with the sunlight.

"Get yourself dressed. But please take a shower and shave that crap off of your face," Priest said, lifting Aja out of her bassinet. "Got my niece up here in the darkness. Tell your daddy you wanna see some daylight," Priest said, smiling at his three-month-old niece.

"Come on, Priest, man, what are you doing? I don't feel like—"

"Dallas, did I ask you anything? I *told* you to get dressed. Now, scat."

Dallas knew better than to argue with his brother so he retreated upstairs and cleaned himself up. Thirty minutes later he ambled downstairs and took a seat on the sofa.

"Listen, little brother, Yasmin's not coming back. I know it's hard on you right now, but do you think she would want you to have her baby cooped up in this place all day? It's nice outside and I'm spending the day with my niece," Priest said as he rubbed noses with the pretty baby girl.

"Well, you just take her out for a few. I'll be a'ight."

"No, I left you alone for three months. That was plenty of time for you to get outta your funk. Now, come on."

"Priest, man . . ."

"*Priest, man* nothing. And you're gonna start dating again too. You'll feel better if you bust a nut every now and then."

"Man, I ain't thinking about no woman."

"And that, my brother, is a problem. You need to start so you can get some circulation going on. Now, let's roll."

Priest took them out to lunch at a fancy restaurant in midtown. After that they went bowling. That was the first time Dallas had smiled since Yasmin passed. After that day he slowly but surely made his reentry into society. Then he mistakenly starting dating again before he was really ready. He'd go out with a young lady and have to force himself to have a good time. Even smiling was a challenge. It didn't matter how cute or intelligent or together the young lady sitting across from him was, she wasn't Yasmin, therefore she wasn't right for him. On one particular night, he was with this young lady named Michelle and they were having sex. But when he looked down at her he saw Yasmin's face. That was it. He abruptly pulled himself up and out of her. He ignored her questions and asked her to leave. Once she was out of his house he retreated back into his shell.

Over the next two years he channeled all of his energy into his daughter and his work. Then he had the misfortune of running across the likes of Kenya Greer.

BALDHEAD, WHO sat beside Dallas in the rear of the car, cursing the police the entire time, snapped Dallas back to the here and now.

"I can't stand y'all funky asses. You know damn well Dallas ain't done nuttin. This is just the white man's way to keep a brother in chains. Ya stankin' bastards! If y'all can't find a real reason to lock us down, then ya make one up. I'mma kill every last one of y'all when I get out. Won't be no more police. We'll have to use firemen to help people. And Lewis, you ought to be ashamed of yo self. How you gonna be a cop? That's a new-age overseer!"

"Well, Mario, that makes you a new-age slave. I want you to put me out of business. Stop robbing folks, stop smoking crack, get a job, and stop being a burden on society," Sergeant Lewis said, turning around in his seat.

Buzz Cut chuckled and took out his notepad to add a few more charges to Baldhead's already extensive list of infractions.

"Oh, you kiss my ass, you house nigga. I ain't never robbed no damn body and I smoke crack cuz I like to smoke crack. You drink liquor, I get high, so what's the difference? We both get fucked up. You see, it's hypocrites like you that make me sick. That's why I'mma blow this whole damn city up when I get out. I know Saddam Bin Laden personally."

Buzz Cut added making terrorist threats to the list.

Dallas shot Baldhead a look.

"What? That's my potna," Baldhead said with a straight face. "We used to fuck hos together over on Bankhead. Until he started growing that fucked-up beard." Baldhead shook his head at the sad memory of days long ago. "That's when it went downhill."

Dallas knew what Baldhead was doing. He was trying to keep his mind off of his troubles by making as much noise as he could. Even if it meant digging his own grave a little deeper. But it was a lost cause; Dallas's mind was stuck on being labeled a rapist, the one crime that even in his huge heart he felt was unforgivable. To him rapists were beyond redemption, because the victims had to live with the fact that they were violated.

Sergeant Lewis wouldn't allow Buzz Cut to put any handcuffs on Dallas, so he was free to bite his nails to help relieve a little stress, a bad habit that carried over from childhood.

The Crown Victoria turned off of Memorial Drive into a tunnel behind the jail. As they waited for a corrections officer to open the gate, a crowd of reporters came running up to the car, yelling questions through the closed window.

"Looks like someone called the dogs," Sergeant Lewis said.

Dallas's heart skipped a beat. *God, why is this happening to me?* he thought. He didn't try to hide from the reporters but he didn't make eye contact with them either. He noticed the same female reporter who'd interviewed him two weeks ago, hailing him as an educational messiah. Now she was shouting at him through the closed window.

"Mr. Dupree, why did you do it?"

Why did I do it? Whatever happened to did I do it?

That's when it came crashing down on him. He was guilty already. In some people's eyes he was a rapist.

"Dallas, I want you to stay close by me when we get inside," Baldhead whispered.

"Man, I don't think I'm going to have a choice where I go."

"They gotta process us and that takes time. You just stay close to me. They got some assholes up in there who'll shank you just 'cause you dressed nice. Stand by me."

The car rolled away from the reporters and stopped in an underground parking garage. Sergeant Lewis and Buzz Cut got out and walked away. A few minutes later Sergeant Lewis came and opened Dallas's door.

"Priest just called and he wanted me to tell you he's already gotten bail set up. So, you should be out of here in about an hour," Sergeant Lewis said.

"What about me?" Baldhead said.

"No, we're gonna keep you awhile. A few feds might wanna talk to you about Saddam Bin Laden or whoever it is you been fucking hos with."

"Come on, Lewis, you know I was just playing with y'all."

"Yeah, that's your problem. You're too old to play so much."

Dallas got out of the car. He looked to his right and noticed a large steel door with a glass slat. Inside he could see a bunch of black faces and he knew he was in jail.

He thanked God for Priest. Pride no longer mattered. And his distaste for his brother's occupation had all but dissipated. Right now all he wanted was to get home to his daughter.

Two uniformed guards came over and led Dallas and Baldhead into a steel vestibule and ordered them to face the wall. They were searched and told to wait. After about five minutes they were led to another area where they were fingerprinted and photographed. Dallas kept a straight face but Baldhead smiled.

"Damn, those some nice shoes, playboy," someone said to Dallas as they were ushered into a holding cell. "What size those is?"

Dallas ignored the guy. He quickly decided that as long as no one laid a hand on him, they were cool. But Baldhead knew what prisoners thought of those who didn't respond.

"They yo size, now try to take 'em," Baldhead barked. "And I promise you I will break my foot off up in your ass."

"Man, I wasn't even talking to you," the man snapped back, looking at Baldhead's run-down shoes. "You can believe that."

"I was talking to you," Baldhead said, getting in the thug's face. "And if you say one more word to me or my little brother, I'mma catch a capital murder, cuz I'mma choke the living shit out of ya."

The man twisted his lips and fanned Baldhead away.

Dallas wanted to leave. He wasn't cut out for the kill-or-be-killed lifestyle of those behind bars. He wasn't scared, but he could think of a million other places he'd rather be. The holding tank held at least two hundred people and it seemed all of them were screaming at the top of their lungs about something. He sat down on a bench and leaned against the wall. His mind drifted to the last time he felt trapped.

DALLAS WAS already six years old when he first felt the beautiful sensation of being loved. From birth until then he had been tossed around from one government housing agency to another. Then out of the blue one day a nice man named Mr. Johnny and his wife, Mrs. Etta, came to the group home where he was housed and said he was coming home with them.

Dallas remembered walking into the huge house thinking that he was dreaming, and what a wonderful dream it was. He thought he had died and gone to heaven. For the first time in his life he had his own room. There was a television set in there, and a Nintendo entertainment center with more arcade games than he could count. He had new clothes and brand-new shoes in the closet waiting for him. His new parents were church folks. Mr. Johnny went every now and then, but Mrs. Etta could be found praising His name from one Monday through to the next. Naturally Dallas gravitated toward Mr. Johnny, and they became real close in a short amount of time. Mr. Johnny took him everywhere. Baseball, basketball, and football games wouldn't start without the two of them sitting side by side. Mr. Johnny loved Dallas like he was his real son. One day while Mr. Johnny was at work, Mrs. Etta made Dallas go to church with her. He was told to stay in the sanctuary, but telling him that was like telling him to roam as he pleased. Dallas played in the aisles until he got bored, then he ventured to the back of the church. His heart dropped in his chest when he saw Mrs. Etta in a compromising position. At six years old most kids don't know what sex is, but growing up around the element he had, he was fully aware of what Mrs. Etta was doing bent over a counter grunting and panting like a dog. Her dress was hiked up around her waist while some man, whom Dallas had seen around the church a few times, bounced up and down behind her. Dallas covered his mouth and ran back out front and took a seat. He had to tell Mr. Johnny what he'd seen. He loved him too much to let that lady do that to him. The first time he had Mr. Johnny alone he told him what he'd seen.

Mr. Johnny just stared at him after Dallas finished his story. It was like he was hoping the words could go back into his new son's mouth. After a few minutes of staring at Dallas, he dropped his head and a tear made its way down his face. Then he stood up and rubbed Dallas's head. He grabbed both sides of his face and smiled down at him. He didn't say anything but Dallas knew things would never be the same. That's when he wished he would've kept his mouth closed. The next day Mr. Johnny was gone. Literally! He committed suicide in the bathroom. A single gunshot wound to the head. No good-bye, no nothing, just gone.

That was the beginning of Dallas's descent into hell. Two days after Mr. Johnny moved on, he and Mrs. Etta were on a Greyhound bus headed to Atlanta. They stayed with her relatives for a few weeks, and after that they moved from one homeless shelter to the next. From one abandoned house to the next.

Dallas was always a talkative child; he never met a stranger. That personality trait was not good for the street life. You needed to know how to keep secrets in order to survive, but he was only seven years old. So in order to keep their life a secret, Mrs. Etta tied Dallas up before she went out. She told him she was looking for work. There would be days at a time when he didn't eat. Sometimes he would break free and search the house for food, and when he didn't find any, he roamed the neighborhood asking neighbors for food. Mrs. Etta would find him.

Crack. The sound of her belt hitting his bony frame. *Crack.* "Didn't I tell you to stay put?" *Crack.* "How did you get loose anyway?" *Crack.* She would beat him until he couldn't cry any more.

Then late one night Priest and Antoine showed up and it was over. He was back in the hands of one of God's children.

11

I'LL BE A'IGHT

*C*armen grabbed the phone before it could finish its first ring. "Hello," she huffed.

Today had been one disaster after another. She had just made the long trip over to Dallas's neighborhood to pick up Aja only to find that her little niece wasn't there. And until the phone rang, she had been pacing around the living room worried sick about Dallas and Kameka.

"Hey, Aunt Carmen," Kameka said tentatively.

"Where are you?"

"At a friend's."

"A friend's? What friend? And how did you get to that friend's house from school? And why did you leave school like that?"

Carmen rattled off questions like an auctioneer. Kameka didn't respond.

"Hello? I'm talking to you."

Again, nothing from Kameka.

"Kameka?"

"Yes," she said softly.

"Where are you?"

"I'm at a friend's," Kameka said.

"Where?"

"Around my way."

"I just called Laquita's, and she said she hasn't seen you."

Kameka was silent. Carmen thought she heard a sniffle.

"I went over there, but she didn't answer the door. I saw her look out the window so I know she was there," Kameka said, her voice cracking.

Carmen pressed her ear to the phone as close as it would go. She was trying to figure out if her niece was crying.

"I'm on my way to pick you up right now. Just tell me where you are."

"You don't have to do that, Aunt Carmen. I mean, I know you're good people but I'll be a'ight."

"What do you mean you'll be all right?"

"I'm gonna stay with my friends for a minute."

"Kameka, I know you think you're old enough to make these kinds of decisions, but you're not. Tell me where you are."

"I just called to tell you that I appreciate what you tried to do and even though I didn't stay at the school long I learned a lot."

"Stay long? Kameka, you didn't even stay for a full day."

"I know, but maybe that was all I needed. I'll be over there some time this weekend to get my things."

"Kameka . . ." Carmen realized that her niece had already made up her mind. "I don't want you to try and do this on your own. Life is not that easy. Let me be there for you."

"You already have. I mean, I know sending me to that school had to cost you a grip. I didn't see anything but Benzes, Beemers, and Jags, and that was just in the student parking lot."

"Okay," Carmen said, thinking she knew what was really bothering her niece. "If it's the school you're worried about, then you don't have a problem because the girl you got into it with has withdrawn."

"It's not that, but I'm straight. I'll talk to you later, Aunt Carmen."

"So, you're just going to quit school?"

"I never said I was quitting. Just taking some time for me."

"Kameka, this is not going to solve anything."

"Bye, Aunt Carmen."

"Kameka! Kameka!" Carmen called out. Then she heard a dial tone.

"Damn it," Carmen said as she slammed the phone down on its base. She scrolled through the caller ID looking for the last incoming call, but Kameka had called from a private number.

Carmen dialed 911 and explained her situation but was told that she couldn't file a missing person report until the person in question was missing for at least forty-eight hours. And even then Carmen couldn't file it because she wasn't the legal guardian. She called Laquita. Bruce answered.

"Who dis?" he said.

"Hello, may I speak with Laquita?"

"Who dis?"

"This is Carmen."

"She ain't talking right now."

"What do you mean she is not talking right now? Tell her to come to the phone. This is about her daughter."

"Nah."

"What?" Carmen said.

"You be easy," Bruce said before hanging up.

Carmen placed the phone back in its base, closed her eyes, and counted to fifty. When she opened her eyes, Sterling was standing in front of her.

"You okay?"

"No," Carmen said.

"What's going on?"

"It's Kameka. She quit school and now she claims she's staying at a friend's house."

"Didn't she just start school today?"

"Yes, but now she says she's not going back."

"What are you going to do?"

"She wouldn't tell me where she is."

"She's probably around her old neighborhood. You wanna ride over there?"

"Yes," Carmen croaked out.

Sterling wrapped his arms around his wife and held her close.

Carmen laid her head on his chest and allowed the rhythm of his heartbeat to calm her. Sterling was just what the doctor ordered. He was always there for her at the right time. She closed her eyes and thanked God for her husband.

"We better go," Carmen said.

They headed out the door and Sterling jumped into the driver's seat of Carmen's car.

"Where is your car?"

"I had to drop it off at the shop," Sterling lied. Actually, he'd sold it, and for less than half its value. It was either that or have his gambling bookies break a few limbs. Even after he sold his car he was still short with their money.

* * *

AS THEY headed over to Carver Homes, Sterling looked over at his wife and wanted to tell her about his current financial situation, but couldn't bring himself to do it. How would she react? What would she think of him? Would she ask him to leave? All of these questions racked his brain as he maneuvered through traffic. He knew he'd find another job, but when? Where? And at the rate the economy was turning, at what wage? This week he had sent out over one hundred résumés, and he would keep sending them until he found legitimate work, but until then he had to pray that lady luck would find him.

Carmen's cell phone rang. It was Priest.

"Did you get him?" she asked.

"Not yet. Still waiting. How are you holding up?"

"I'm hanging in there."

"Did you get Aja?"

"I went over there to get her but Mrs. Morton said her grandmother had already picked her up."

"Dallas must've called her from the jail."

"I wish he would've told me. I could've saved a trip."

"How's Kameka doing?"

Carmen sighed. "Well, not too good," she said and ran through the latest crisis for Priest. "We're headed over there right now to see if Laquita knows anything."

"Teenagers," Priest cracked. "Let me know if you need me."

"You call me when you get Dallas."

"I'll do it. Oh, and Carmen? I need to talk to you once we get this mess straightened out."

"About what?" Carmen asked cautiously. Inexplicably her heart started to race. Priest wasn't the kind of man to engage in idle chatter, so when he called a conference it was serious business and almost never good news.

"It's about your husband," he said.

The way he said "your husband" frightened Carmen. She knew what world Priest operated in and found herself wondering what in the world Priest could possibly know about her husband.

12

MORE TROUBLE

*I*t was one thirty in the morning when Dallas walked out of the Atlanta City Jail. Eight hours of hanging around the worst folks Atlanta had to offer had depressed the hell out of him. Although he was now a free man, his stomach remained in knots. The minute the guard pushed the button to open the large steel door to the lobby, he was ambushed.

"Mr. Dupree, can I have a word with you?" a reporter asked, shoving a microphone in his face.

Dallas stopped and a bright light from a news camera almost blinded him.

"I'm not a rapist. It's not in my character to do what I've been accused of. I'm innocent."

"Do you care to explain what happened?"

"That's all I'm going to say for now."

A few more questions were shouted at him as he

walked out of the building. He raced up the stairs, searching for Carmen's car. When he didn't see it he walked across the street to use the phone. That's when he heard a car horn. As he turned around, a Mercedes pulled in front of him and stopped. The passenger window rolled down.

"Get in," Priest said.

Dallas hadn't seen his brother since Carmen's wedding but he didn't hesitate to climb into the car. He jumped in the passenger side and the seat belt automatically wrapped itself around him.

"How ya doing, little bro?"

Dallas opened his mouth to respond but at first nothing came out. He was still in shock. Eight hours in a rat hole had taken something away from him.

"I'm all right," Dallas managed.

Priest sat quietly and let his little brother have a moment. He patted Dallas's leg, then drove away.

"This is a nice car, man," Dallas said, looking around the luxury automobile.

"Only about fifty made this year."

"I guess life is treating you well."

"Not bad."

"Why, Priest?" Dallas asked out of the blue. He loved his brother to no end but he just couldn't understand why he chose to be a drug dealer.

"Life," Priest said, slowly turning the wheel as the car glided on to Ashby Street.

Dallas knew Priest wasn't a big talker. He chose his words carefully and left it up to the listener to read between the lines. But he expected more than that.

"Priest?"

"Yeah?"

"Can you bail Baldhead out? They locked him up when they arrested me. He was looking out for me. Got in about three fights."

"Fuck Mario."

"Come on, man, he was looking out for me."

"Then you bail him out."

Dallas sighed and decided to let it go. Even though he never wanted to see the Atlanta Detention Center, he would go and get Baldhead.

Priest pulled up into Dallas's driveway and slid his car into park.

"Thanks, man," Dallas said.

"You got it."

"You're always coming through for me."

"You're family," Priest responded.

"Even before I was family you were there," Dallas said softly. "Yo, man, I'm sorry about the way I've been acting towards you lately. I'm not your judge, and what you do is not my business, so like I said, I apologize for tripping on you. If you wanna be a drug dealer then so be it."

Priest looked at Dallas and nodded his head. "Just remember this, little bro: Things aren't always as bad as they seem."

"Yeah, well, it seems like I'm in a world of trouble right now," Dallas said, leaning his head back into the headrest. He wanted to cry and purge himself of all the hell life had thrown his way but he held it in.

Priest reached over and rubbed his brother's back.

"How do I always end up with the bad luck?"

"Don't know. And you shouldn't spend too much time wallowing in it. It is what it is. Deal with it."

Dallas looked at his brother. He didn't know why he even bothered to say anything. It wasn't like he was looking for pity. Just wanted an ear. Priest's response let him know he would've had more of an ear if he'd been talking to a stray dog.

"Dallas, you're soft and that's what most folks look for when they are searching for a victim. You're too damn nice," Priest spat disgustedly. "And you don't think."

"What?"

"You ain't no Kobe Bryant, but it's pretty damn obvious that you got some money. And that's the one thing women look for in a man. Damn all that Dr. Phil emotional bullshit. A woman wants a man to take care of her. Even if they can pay their own way, they still want the protection of a man, and as you can tell, some of 'em can go to great lengths when they can't get what they want."

Dallas was surprised by the tone and stared at his brother.

"You better get a set of nuts or you'll forever be in some shit. Now, whoever this girl is would've never said no shit like this about me."

"How do you even know what happened, Priest?" Dallas asked.

Priest gave him a look to let him know that he already had the scoop on why he was arrested.

"And do you know why? Cuz there's a helluva consequence for crossing me. You . . . You just let folks run all over you."

"No I don't."

"Yes you do." Priest reached over and backhanded Dallas in the side of his face.

Dallas frowned and instinctively balled up his fist.

"Man what the—" he said.

"You see what I'm talking about?" Priest said, slamming his hand on the steering wheel. "You trynna talk. Hit me in my damn face and we'll talk *after* I get my foot out of your ass. *After.* You know what *after* means, don't you?"

Dallas tried to open the door but it was locked.

"Sit still."

"Man, fuck you. Do I look like a child to you?" Dallas barked. "You think because you hit me and I didn't react like you would that I'm soft?

Nah, I didn't hit you back because I respect you and you're the only father I've ever known, but make no mistake about it, you raise your hand to me again and we gonna solve some problems the only way you seem to understand."

Priest looked out of the driver's side window. A few minutes of silence passed.

"You know what? You're right," Priest said. "My bad."

"Unlock this door, man," Dallas said, still pissed and not wanting to hear Priest's half-hearted apology.

"Gimme a hug," Priest teased. This was vintage Priest. He always tried to calm down a situation with a joke.

"Open this door, man."

"Come on, baby brah, I miss you," Priest said with a wide grin. "Give big bro a hug."

That's when it hit Dallas. Priest was like the father who was mad with his son for falling out of the tree. His anger came because he loved him too much to see him hurt.

Dallas turned away from the door and backhanded Priest with a left hand that caught him right on his forehead. Priest grabbed Dallas's hand and started twisting it before he caught himself.

"Boy, you hit like a little bitch. Mina hit harder than that."

"Get off me," Dallas said, snatching his hand back. "And why is Mina hitting you?"

"We're freaky like that. She likes to slap my ass when I hit missionary style."

Dallas shook his head. "You got issues."

"A'ight, we're even," Priest said, frowning and rubbing his forehead. "Damn, Dallas, that hurt."

"Yeah, you do it again and I'mma—"

"You ain't gonna do nothing."

Dallas felt good hanging out with his brother. He hadn't felt this way in a long time. But the good feelings quickly disappeared when he remembered why his brother was there.

"Dallas, I want you to listen to me. There are two ways we can handle this situation. We can get you the best lawyer money can buy and fight it out in the courts or . . ." Priest smiled. "Or I can handle it."

Dallas visualized Kenya Greer with a bullet in her head, floating in the Chattahoochee River. He saw her little boy at the funeral and shook the picture from his head. He knew right away he couldn't let Priest take care of it. It just wasn't in him to go down that road.

Priest must've been reading Dallas's mind because he shook his head in a way that said *I told you you were soft.*

"Listen, little bro. I know you didn't do what they said you did. Everyone who knows you knows you didn't do what they said you did. This is yet another one of life's puzzles. We'll figure it out and we'll be okay."

Dallas wanted to believe his brother but he didn't trust his fate in a court of law. He knew one too many innocent people who had been shackled and shipped away to those modern-day plantations that society called prisons. But he couldn't go the route Priest wanted to take either.

"That's why I stay to myself," Dallas said. "Why would anybody lie about something like this?"

"Human beings are strange creatures. Women are even stranger. So, who is this girl?"

"Some substitute teacher who works at my school."

"I already know that much. Did you have sex with her?"

"I guess."

"What do you mean, you guess? You did or you didn't."

"I don't remember, man. All I know is I got drunk and passed out. When I woke up I was at her house, naked."

"So, you don't remember having sex with her?"

"Nah."

"Then what makes you think you did?"

"Because I saw a used condom on the floor when I got dressed."

"How do you know it was yours? She might be a freak and just didn't clean up after herself."

"Why didn't the police ask those questions before they arrested me?"

"Because when you go to jail this country can function. Prisons are big business. Now, when did you start drinking?"

"That was the first and last time," Dallas said, trying his best to remember every detail of that night's episode. The memories stopped at Café Intermezzo.

"Okay, I want you to go in the house and get some rest. We'll get this behind us soon enough. You'll be okay."

"Can I borrow your cell phone? I need to check up on Aja. Let her know I'm alright."

"Sure, but it's a little late to be calling those people's house, don't you think?"

"What people? She's with Carmen."

"Carmen said Aja's grandmother picked her up."

Dallas's heart almost jumped out of his chest.

"Aw, damn," Dallas said as he fiddled with Priest's door. He heard a light click and the door opened. He ran to his truck.

"What's going on?" Priest shouted.

"I don't want Aja over there."

"Why?"

"Mrs. Gibson is getting a little crazy. She already cut off all my baby's hair. Thanks, man, for looking out. I'll call you later," Dallas said over his shoulder. He got into his truck and started it, and before Priest could move, Dallas had already driven across his immaculate lawn, leaving twenty-four-inch tire trails in his wake.

13

SHE A PIMP

"What's going on with you?" Carmen snapped at Sterling as he pulled into the parking lot at Carver Homes. She had planned to wait until they had taken care of Kameka before mentioning anything, but she just couldn't hold it in any longer.

"What do you mean?" Sterling asked.

"My brother just said he wanted to talk to me about you. Now, is there anything you would like to tell me?"

Sterling paused. "Carmen, I have no idea what your brother could want to talk to you about."

"Sterling, I know we only dated for six months before we got married, but the one thing I felt in my heart was that I could trust you. Now, please be straight with me. What's going on?"

Sterling hesitated and let out a long sigh before speaking. "I lost my job."

"Okay . . ." Carmen said, motioning with her hand for him to tell her more.

"And I sold my car so that I could help out with the bills."

Carmen stared at her husband, unsure of what to think. There had to be more to the story or Priest wouldn't have sounded so urgent. But then again, Priest made a big deal out of everything when it came to her and Dallas. She remembered how he had always been so protective of her, especially when it came to guys. And he'd never cared for Sterling.

The more she thought about it, the calmer she felt.

"Carmen, I didn't know how to tell you so I figured I could ride this thing out until I found another job."

"Is that why you were borrowing money from your brother?"

"Yeah," Sterling said, lowering his head. "I just didn't know what else to do."

"Oh, baby," Carmen said, rubbing his hand. "What made you think you'd have to hide something like that from me?"

Sterling slowly shook his head and hunched his shoulders.

"We're a team, baby," Carmen said, "and trust me when I say, I'm not under any delusion that the rest of our lives will be peaches and cream. People lose their jobs every day and that's nothing to be ashamed of."

"You're right. I think something might be in the works. I have a few interviews set up for next week."

Carmen patted his leg and breathed a sigh of relief. She thought Priest was going to shatter her world by telling her Sterling was seeing another woman. This job crap was nothing. This she could deal with.

"Let's go and find my niece," she said, exiting the car.

As they made their way through the dilapidated buildings toward Laquita's house, Carmen noticed the same young man she'd sprayed with mace walking toward her.

"Excuse me. Can I talk to you for a minute?"

Carmen thought the boy had completely lost his mind. It was one thing to harass her when she was alone, but another thing altogether to approach her when she was with her husband.

"Young man, I don't have time for your games," Carmen said, stepping around the youngster.

"It's about Meek. I mean Kameka."

Carmen stopped dead in her tracks, causing Sterling to bump into her back.

"What do you know about Kameka?" Carmen said, turning around and walking back toward the boy.

"She's making some bad moves," he said, shaking his head. "Some real bad moves."

"What are you talking about?"

"She running around with Kitty and her crew."

"Who is Kitty?" Carmen asked.

"She a pimp."

"A what?"

"A pimp. I saw Meek with her earlier and that surprised me cuz that ain't like Meek."

"Where can I find this Kitty lady?"

"Oh, you don't wanna go 'round there without some backup. Kitty play for keeps. She ain't no joke."

"Where is she?" Sterling spoke up. "I think we can handle it from there."

"Brah," the boy said, sizing Sterling up. "I ain't gonna even play y'all like that. Unless y'all got a ton of guns and a ghetto pass, y'all better choose another course of action. Cuz if y'all run up on them plain Jane, it could get ugly."

Carmen's frustration was obvious. She was tempted to get in her car and leave all of this ghetto foolishness to the natives. She thought about the many late nights she had stayed up studying her med books, all of the cramming for tests, all of the sacrifices she had made to leave this life, and for what? To try and save a little girl who didn't want to be saved. But there was something else pulling at her to stay the course. Maybe it was Antoine talking to her.

"What is your name?"

"They call me Psycho."

"Well, Psycho, I really appreciate the information," Carmen said, reaching in her purse and removing a ten-dollar bill. She offered it to him but he looked at her like he was offended.

"This ain't about that. You just get Meek straight. She one of the good ones. Trust me on that," he said before walking away.

Carmen felt smaller than she had ever felt. Feeling frustrated, she marched down to Laquita's house with Sterling on her heels.

Carmen knocked on the door and Bruce answered.

"What up," he said, looking at Carmen like she was Sunday's dinner. Then he looked at Sterling and did a double take. He smiled and his face lit up with recognition. "What up, hustler?"

Sterling looked like he wanted to run out of his skin.

"Boy, I ain't seen you in a long time," Bruce said, opening the door and grabbing Sterling's hand.

Sterling nodded his head but showed no sign of knowing Bruce. Carmen could tell he was giving Bruce some kind of eye signal, because Bruce said, "What? Oh . . . okay," nodding his head when not a word ever left Sterling's mouth.

"Where do you know him from?" Carmen asked.

"We grew up together," Sterling lied. "Ain't that right, Bruce?"

"Yeah," Bruce said, doing a piss-poor acting job.

"Um-huh," Carmen said, staring at her husband warily. She decided not to make a big deal out of Sterling and Bruce's acquaintance, because on any given day, she could bump into someone she knew who still lived in Georgia's projects.

"Where is Laquita?" she asked Bruce.

"Baby!" Bruce called out. "She doesn't do nothing but sleep. I hope she ain't pregnant."

"For the child's sake, let's hope not," Carmen said.

Laquita appeared wearing the same bathrobe she wore the last time Carmen saw her, only now it wasn't wrapped so tightly around her. Her ample cleavage was sticking out for the world to see.

"Cover yourself up, Laquita," Carmen said.

"Did you forget where you at? This is my house and if I wanna walk around butt-ass naked I can," Laquita said, throwing open her robe so that both of her huge breasts were exposed.

Carmen shook her head. This girl was beyond repair, she thought.

"Have you heard anything from Kameka?"

"Nope," Laquita said, lighting up a cigarette.

"She said she came by here but you wouldn't let her in," Carmen said.

"Maybe I wasn't home."

"Could've been at work, huh?"

"You know what? You agreed to take Kameka, so as far as I'm concerned, she's yo problem. You seeing how she really is now, ain't ya?"

"No, what I'm seeing is a brilliant little girl who had the misfortune of being born to a ghettofied, ignorant-ass nigger like you," Carmen snapped. She was at the end of her rope.

Laquita smiled.

"Oh, shucks. Carmen got a little spunk," Laquita said, not in the least bit offended. "On the real though, I gotta get my sleep. I ain't seen the little girl but if she come by I'll give you a call." Laquita finally closed her robe.

"Laquita, do you even care what happens to her? I hear she's running around with a pimp."

"She's damn near grown. By the time I was her age I had her and was living on my own. She can make her own decisions in life. Now if y'all will excuse me, I gotta get my rest. See yourself out," Laquita said and disappeared around the corner to her room.

Carmen stood there in total shock. For the life of her she couldn't figure out how someone could carry a child for forty weeks, raise that child for sixteen years, then discard her in a matter of minutes like she was a used napkin.

"Let's go," Carmen said to Sterling.

"Sterl, we need to talk, baby boy. I heard you back in the game," Bruce said, opening up the door.

Carmen saw the scornful look Sterling shot at Bruce. Then he almost knocked her over getting out of the place. Something wasn't right.

14

GOING CRAZY

*D*allas sped up to Mrs. Gibson's house and slammed his truck into park. He opened the door and hit the ground running. With one thrust of his long legs, he leaped up the four steps to the porch and banged on the wooden screen door.

"Who is it?" Mrs. Gibson asked, her voice weighed down with concern.

"It's Dallas," he said, almost out of breath.

"Who?" she said.

"Dallas."

"Wait a minute," Mrs. Gibson said.

Dallas could hear her rumbling around the house. Then Mrs. Gibson walked out onto the porch and pulled the door behind her.

"Where's Aja?" Dallas said.

"She's asleep," Mrs. Gibson whispered, looking around Dallas as if someone had run around the corner of her house.

"Mrs. Gibson, I appreciate you picking her up, but that wasn't necessary," Dallas said.

"Dallas, who out here with you?"

Dallas looked around. "Nobody."

"Did you hear that?"

"Mrs. Gibson, can you get Aja for me? It's late and I'm kind of tired."

"I heard about what happened to you on the news and I was just concerned about my baby. There is no need for all the hostility."

"Mrs. Gibson, there is no hostility in my voice. I'm just trying to pick up my baby."

"Well, no."

"No? What do you mean, no?"

"I think it's best she stays here while you're in jail."

"Mrs. Gibson, how can I be in jail if I'm standing right here?"

"I don't know. Did you break out?"

Dallas looked at the old lady, who was still looking around as if she were hearing voices. There was no way he was leaving his daughter in her care.

"You sit tight," Mrs. Gibson said, disappearing back into the house. She closed the door behind her and Dallas heard the locks click into their chambers. He knew then that this wasn't going to go smoothly.

Dallas paced around on the porch, all the while looking at his watch. He saw Mrs. Gibson's blinds move and he wondered what was going on.

Why is the old lady watching me without bringing me my daughter? Dallas thought.

Dallas looked at his watch and realized he had been pacing for almost five minutes. He knew it shouldn't take that long for Mrs. Gibson to get his daughter ready so he banged on the door again.

"Mrs. Gibson! Mrs. Gibson!"

There was no answer. He turned around and saw a set of headlights moving rapidly toward him. He got a sinking feeling in the pit of his stomach.

The white police cruiser came to a screeching halt in front of him and a short Hispanic police officer jumped out.

"Sir, will you come down off of the porch with your hands where I can see them?" he commanded as he positioned himself behind his car.

"No. You go in there and get my daughter."

"Sir, I'm asking you nicely," the police officer said, removing his gun and pointing it at Dallas.

These clowns are so quick to pull their gun on a black man, he thought.

"Are you kidding me?" Dallas said, completely baffled. "I'm not leaving here without my daughter."

The police officer radioed for backup and within a few minutes five more police cars converged on the small house. Lights flashed as officers took their positions.

Dallas couldn't believe what he was seeing. Today had been one long nightmare.

What did this old lady tell these clowns? he wondered.

"Sir, will you step off of the porch with your hands where I can see them?" a different police officer asked.

Dallas didn't move. He wanted to reach into his pocket and grab his cell phone to call Priest but then thought about that brother in New York who was shot forty-one times after reaching for his wallet. For health reasons, he decided against that move.

"What are you going to do? Shoot me because I'm trying to pick up my own child? You should go in there and arrest that damn nutcase she has for a grandmother. That's kidnapping, you know!"

"Sir, put your hands up above your head," the police officer yelled at the top of his lungs.

The porch light came on and the door to the house opened. Mrs. Gibson walked out holding a sleeping Aja. She handed her to Dallas.

"Dallas, what is going on out here?"

"What? You tell me!"

"Here, take your baby," she said wearily as if she hadn't the slightest clue what was going on.

One of the police officers rushed up and pointed a gun at Dallas.

"Ma'am, are you all right?"

"Of course I'm all right. Now you put that gun away on my property."

"Did this gentleman threaten you?"

"No, this boy just here to pick up his child. Why y'all out here this time of night causing trouble?"

"Ma'am, we got a call that there was a breaking and entering in progress."

"Y'all must have the wrong house," Mrs. Gibson admonished.

"Sir, may I see your identification?"

"No," Dallas barked. "Didn't she just tell you you had the wrong house? Is there a law against picking up your own kid?"

"Sir, I'm only doing my job."

"And I'm doing mine," Dallas said, holding his daughter a little closer.

Mrs. Gibson spoke. "Officer, there is nobody breaking in my house. Now why don't y'all go on before my grandbaby wakes up. Dallas ain't bothering nobody."

"Dallas?" the officer said, relaxing his posture. "Are you Dallas Dupree?"

"Why?" Dallas asked, his patience wearing thin.

"I know your brother Priest," he said, finally putting his gun away. "I heard about what happened to you. I'm really sorry to hear that."

"Yeah, well if you'll excuse me, I need to get my daughter home."

"You got it. Sorry about this little mix-up. Tell Priest Billy Thomas asked about him," the officer said, turning around and waving his backup down.

Dallas nodded and walked off the porch and over to his truck.

"Dallas, you call me when you get in," Mrs. Gibson said.

"We'll be fine," he said, making a mental note to make a doctor's appointment for the old lady.

The minute Dallas buckled Aja in her car seat his cell phone rang. He wondered who was calling him at this time of the morning.

The caller ID read Genesis Styles. Genesis was Dallas's old college roommate. The last time he had seen Genesis was at his wedding ceremony when his fiancée Terri had shocked the entire church by showing up in a jogging suit instead of a wedding dress and handing him a baby. Later they found out that Genesis had been creeping around with this young girl who worked at the bookstore that Terri owned.

"What up, Genesis?" Dallas said. He was tired and it was reflected in his voice.

"Dallas. How you doing, man? I was just watching the news and . . ."

"Yeah, I know." Dallas was not in the mood to relive his drama-filled day.

"Is there anything I can do?"

"You know a good lawyer?"

"My sister. She the best."

"Well that's what I need."

"Hold on," Genesis said.

Dallas heard him calling to Terri so he figured they were giving love another try.

"You got a pen?"

"Yeah," Dallas said, looking in his console. "How is Terri doing?"

"She's good. We just got in from Jamaica. A little getaway does the body good, you know?"

"Tell me about it. So y'all working it out, huh?"

"Trying. It's been a long road but we're happy. I had a lot of growing up to do, but anyway . . . when we got in I turned on the news and heard about you. I was like, 'This can't be.'"

"Yeah, well it's not true. I don't know what's going on but this charge is bogus."

"Oh, man, you don't even have to go there with me. I knew it was a lie when I heard it. Here, take this number." Genesis rattled off a few numbers. "If she can't help you, I'm sure she can put you in contact with someone who can. She just got married so her name is Phyllis Pryor now," Genesis said.

"Genesis, I appreciate this, man. I'm going to call her first thing in the morning."

"You do that. And if you need me and Terri to help you out with Aja, just call."

"I appreciate that."

"You got it," Genesis said. "Yo, Dallas?"

"Yeah."

"Keep your head up, brah."

"I'll be a'ight," Dallas said before hanging up. Only he wasn't sure if he believed that.

I LIKE THE WAY YOU MOVE!

Kameka sat on a wobbly stool in front of a cracked vanity mirror framed by blown-out lightbulbs. Her hands shook as she tried to apply some gaudy blue eye shadow.

Second thoughts crept into her mind as she looked around the dark and musty little room at all the girls getting ready for the night shift. Just as she made up her mind to sneak out the back door, Kitty walked in with about five other girls.

"Come on, girl, get a move on," Kitty said, throwing a fake identification card on the table in front of Kameka. "Here is your paperwork. You're twenty-two years old. Now, hurry up. You can't make no money sitting around here looking at yourself in the mirror."

Kameka pulled herself up and walked over to the bag Kitty had given her. She removed a few revealing bathing suits from the duffel bag and closed her eyes.

She couldn't believe what she was doing to herself. She closed her eyes to stop the tears from ruining her makeup.

Kameka stole a look at Kitty to see if she had witnessed her mini-breakdown and realized that she was indeed being watched. Kitty walked over to Kameka and placed a hand on her shoulder.

"You doing all right over here?" Kitty said, showing a rare moment of compassion.

Kameka nodded and tried to act as if everything was fine.

"Listen, Sade," Kitty said, calling Kameka by her new street name. "This takes a little getting used to but you'll be okay. Just act like you're performing for your boyfriend." She gyrated her hips in a seductive fashion. "This is just an act, baby. You selling these horny tricks a dream and the best actress gets the best payday. Remember what I told you about blocking these tricks out?"

Kameka nodded and gave a halfhearted smile.

"Come on, baby, pull it together. You got a slamming body and a cute-ass face. And that, my friend, will get you paid like a muthafucka. Once you see how fast those tricks throw that cheese at you, you'll be asking yourself what took you so long to come and holla at me. Now, you came to me with what you needed and I told you I'd help you get it. Let's do the damn thing," Kitty said, before walking off to motivate another girl.

Kameka twisted her lips at Kitty as she sashayed away. She didn't like Kitty. As a matter of fact she hated her, but for now Kitty was all she had. Her mother didn't want her in her world and there was no place for a kid from the projects in her aunt Carmen's world. So this was it.

She looked at all of the other girls peeling off their already skimpy attire and laughing up a storm.

Kameka took a deep breath and removed her shirt. It took all the strength she could muster not to cry. Next were her jeans. Once she was standing there in her panties and bra she heard laughter behind her. She turned around to see what everyone found so amusing and quickly found out she was the target.

"Girl, you ever heard of thongs? Where you get them big-ass period drawers from?" one girl said, giving the others high fives.

Kameka turned around and ignored the girls. She hated all of them. They were losers who aspired to be nothing more than what they already were. She knew she was different. Or was she?

She removed her panties and bra and quickly slipped into the two-piece bathing suit. She pulled her hair back into a ponytail, slid a garter on her left thigh and slipped her feet into some six-inch-high stilettos.

God knew she didn't plan on being in the business of pleasing men for the rest of her life.

EXPLAIN YOURSELF

"Daddy, are you bad?" Aja asked as Dallas tucked her into his bed.

"No, sweetie. Daddy's not bad," Dallas said softly.

It broke his heart to answer that question.

"Then why did those police take you away?"

Dallas took a deep breath and sat on the side of the bed. He ran his hand across his Aja's forehead and looked down into her innocent eyes. Unlike the kids in his class, she had no idea how the judicial system was set up for people like them. Guilty until proven innocent.

"Well, sweetie, the police are just like everyone else. They make mistakes. And that's what happened with daddy."

"You said God takes care of good people. You're good."

"Yes."

"Daddy, did you make God mad?"

Dallas smiled at his child's persistence.

"No, I didn't make God angry. This one just got by Him."

"How?"

"Well, sweetie, God can be mighty busy sometimes. He has the whole entire world to look after, so every now and then something will get by Him, but He normally finds out and fixes things pretty quick."

"Okay," Aja said, satisfied that the big man upstairs would take care of her father. She rolled onto her side and closed her eyes.

Dallas smiled. It felt so good to be with his daughter. Just a few hours ago, he didn't know if he'd ever see her pretty face again. All kinds of thoughts ran through his head when he was in jail.

THE CHILD MOLESTER who was terrorizing his neighborhood was found and locked up while Dallas was incarcerated. After the inmates discovered who the child molester was, they welcomed him with closed fists and swift kicks. After a good twenty minutes of relentless beatings by any and everyone who ever had a mother, daughter, sister, or aunt, a corrections officer lazily walked over and stopped the rat pack. The man was beaten beyond recognition.

Dallas watched as the man was wheeled away and couldn't help but wonder if the police had arrested the right man. Then he heard someone call for "that teacher rapist." He tensed up. His thoughts immediately went to Aja and his vow to never leave her, but in his heart he knew keeping that vow depended on these clowns, because under no circumstances was he going to end up like their first victim. As the seconds passed, Dallas was introduced to a side of him that he never knew existed. He knew the first person who approached him in a threatening manner would take him from being a rape suspect to a bona fide murderer, because he had all intentions of going for the kill. But he didn't have to worry about that because God was looking out for him in the form of Mario "Baldhead" Jackson.

"Move a muscle towards this man and I'll bury each and every one of you hos. Y'all niggas know what I'm about. So make a move," Baldhead said, standing in front of Dallas like a father lion protecting his pride. "Get a little froggy and jump."

The rat pack kept coming.

Dallas stood up and removed his shirt. The highly defined muscles let the rat pack know they were in for a long night. And after a few tense minutes, they wisely backed down.

"Now, I'm disappointed," Baldhead said. "Here I was all ready to kick a little ass and y'all gonna go and get sensible."

Dallas eased back down onto the hard bench. He maintained a fierce demeanor but inside he hated himself for what he knew he was about to do.

Now would be a good time for Baldhead to shut the hell up, he thought, but he knew better. Baldhead was worked up now and it would be a while before he calmed down.

DALLAS BLINKED the memory from his mind.

"I think you made God mad, Daddy," Aja said with her eyes closed.

"What makes you think that?"

"Cuz you didn't come and get me for lunch."

"Go to sleep," Dallas said, throwing the covers over her head. "I love you."

"I love you too, daddy," Aja said. "Daddy?"

"Yes, Aja," Dallas said, smiling at his talkative little girl. "Are you gonna let daddy get his shower or are you going to talk my ear off?"

"Grandma said you were going to jail for a long time. And that's not true, is it?"

Anger returned and he quickly decided that Aja had visited the Gibson household for the last time. At least until Mrs. Gibson could get some medication for her issues. If Mrs. Gibson wanted to see her granddaughter she would have to venture off of her premises.

"Sweetie, your grandmother is becoming ill. It happens to older people sometimes. Then they start saying things that aren't true."

"How is she sick? Is she crazy?"

Getting there in a hurry, Dallas thought.

"No, she's not crazy. Her memory is getting a little old, that's all, and she can't make good choices right now."

"Is that why she cut my hair?"

"Yes, and I'm sorry about that."

"It's okay, Daddy. Now I look like my mommy."

"Yes, you do," Dallas said, and his eyes immediately went to the drawing of Yasmin.

"Will you lie down with me, Daddy?"

"After I get a quick shower."

Dallas jumped into the shower and hurried back to lie down beside his daughter.

Aja adjusted herself and made Dallas's arm her pillow. Within a matter of minutes she was snoring just like her mother used to do.

Dallas rolled over and kissed his daughter on her tiny lips. He removed Aja's head from his arm and sat up on the side of the bed.

He was nervous. What was he going to do? How would this situation play itself out? He picked up the phone and dialed Kenya's number. He wanted to hear from the horse's mouth why she was railroading him. Her line was busy. There was a stutter tone letting him know that he had messages. He pushed star-nine-eight, and an automated voice announced that he had twenty messages.

The first few messages were from concerned friends. Carmen left about five. Priest left one, but message number thirteen shook him to the core.

"Fuck all y'all. I ain't gonna stop till I ruin the whole bloodline," a voice he didn't recognize barked. "Now that ass is going to prison. I guess you ain't so high and mighty now, huh? Don't drop the soap." The man was laughing now.

Dallas saved the message.

"Dallas, this is Mrs. Locus. First, let me say I'm really sorry to hear about your troubles. Why don't you take a few days off and get your affairs in order? You have all of our support. I want you to know this is just my advice and I'm not saying this in my official capacity as principal of the school. You're not suspended and nothing official has been added to your file. If you want to come to work you're free to do so. God bless you and hang on in there."

Dallas saved that message as well. The next message was from Baldhead.

"Man, don't worry about coming to get me, because I had a few failure-to-appears. So I'm going to have to see the judge in the morning. You make sure you get you a white attorney. This is the South, and when it's all said and done black folks' scared of white people. Hold on, Dallas," Baldhead said, then he snapped at someone in the background. "Nigga, don't you see I'm on the phone? Hell no I ain't got no cigarette. What I look like, the Marlboro man?

"Dallas, I'm back. Oh hell, I done forgot what I was talking about. These niggas in here getting on my nerves. Tell Priest I said to kiss my ass. I know you told him to come and get me and what did he say?"

Baldhead stopped as if Dallas was on the phone to answer him. "Ol' bastard. Anyway, I'm sleepy. So come and check on a brother tomorrow after three."

Dallas shook his head and made a mental note to do just what Baldhead asked of him.

The rest of the messages were the same as the first few, concerned friends.

Dallas looked at the clock on his nightstand and realized it was almost four o'clock in the morning. He walked downstairs and turned on the television. Bad move. The first face he saw was his.

"A popular teacher was arrested yesterday on sexual assault charges. Dallas Dupree, well known for his active involvement in the enhancement and revitalization of the West End area of Atlanta, was arrested without incident in front of his home. Area residents were shocked when they heard the news."

Dallas recognized all of his neighbors as they jockeyed for TV time. All of them said positive things about him and he appreciated it.

He hit the mute button and leaned his head back on his plush sofa. He had almost drifted off to sleep when his doorbell rang. He flipped the remote to the channel that engaged his gate cam. It was Daddy-O, Mrs. Morton's husband.

Dallas jumped up and hurried to the door. He loved Daddy-O like a grandfather. Mr. Morton was the man who'd convinced him to invest in real estate. Not just any real estate, West End real estate. They went into business together buying and rehabbing all of the older homes in his area, and so far, they had bought and sold almost one hundred homes.

"BLACK FOLKS are where it's at, young man," Ozell "Daddy-O" Morton said as he walked up to Dallas and introduced himself on the day

Dallas moved into the neighborhood. "Ozell Morton's my name. Welcome to the neighborhood."

Daddy-O was a well-dressed and meticulous man. His dark brown face was clean shaven and looked like it had never housed a pimple, but the most striking thing about Daddy-O was his hair. Grey dreadlocks extended all the way down to just below his knees.

"Dallas Dupree. Nice to meet you," Dallas said, extending his hand.

"And who might this bundle of joy be?"

"That's my daughter, Aja," Dallas said proudly.

"How old is she?"

"Three months."

"Ohhhh, you're in trouble. This little girl is gonna have you in the palm of her hand."

"She already does."

Daddy-O smiled as if Aja was his own child.

"You married?"

Dallas shook his head and his eyes automatically betrayed him. Daddy-O seemed to sense that this was a sore subject and moved the conversation right along.

"I love to see black folks moving in instead of out. You have no idea how much it hurts my soul to see us running from each other."

"Well, this is the place my fiancée said she wanted. So I bought it. Got a great deal on it too."

"That's good. Well, I'm sure she'll fix it up right nice."

"She passed away," Dallas eased out.

"Oh," Daddy-O said. "I'm so sorry to hear that." Warmth and sincerity emanated from his eyes, soothing Dallas and helping him to return to the present.

Dallas nodded his appreciation.

"Well, Mr. Dupree, I'm going to let you get back to moving. My wife will probably bring you a pie or a cake or something," he said, nodding across the street to his house. "That's just how she is."

"Sounds like my kind of neighbor."

"Her name is Mattie and I'll let you know right now you're going to have a time keeping her away from this little angel right here." Daddy-O nodded toward Aja.

Dallas smiled.

"You go on and get settled in. We'll have plenty of time to get acquainted with each other."

And get acquainted they did. Dallas found out that Daddy-O had spent forty-one years on the bench before he retired as a Georgia Supreme Court justice. They spent many days and evenings talking to each other about life. Daddy-O never had any kids and Dallas never had a father, so they filled a mutual void for each other. They spent so much time together that Mrs. Mattie started calling Dallas her son.

"DALLAS," DADDY-O called out from the street.

Dallas clicked open the gate and stood in the doorway while Daddy-O strolled up the walkway and onto the porch.

"Pardon the hour, but I was worried about you."

"No problem," Dallas said, trying to sound upbeat. He knew no matter how severe the stress level, Daddy-O didn't host pity parties, nor did he attend them.

"It's a pretty night. Let's talk out here," Daddy-O said as he walked over and took a seat in the rocking chair.

Dallas walked out onto the porch. He took in a deep whiff of the cool Atlanta night air and immediately felt better.

"Are you all right?"

"Yeah." Dallas sighed.

"Well, Mattie 'bout crazy with worry over there. When she called and told me they came and got you, my old ticker almost gave out. What's going on?"

"I wish I knew. I'm just as confused about this whole thing as anyone else."

"You know, Dallas, life can be cruel at times. Just when we think we're on cruise control, good old life throws a big pothole for us to maneuver around."

"Tell me about it."

"You're a good man, Dallas. I knew that the first time I spoke with you. And I know this . . . sexual assault thing is not you, but . . . we have to deal with it. Have you secured an attorney yet?"

"First thing in the morning. I just got home not too long ago."

"Yeah, well, make sure you spare no expense. This is your freedom you're talking about and I don't have to tell you that little girl needs you. So don't go in half-cocked. Go with the best money can buy. The courts are just like anywhere else. They respond to power. I can't count the number of judges I know personally who are in awe of the Johnnie Cochrans of the world. Now, they won't admit it, but it's a fact."

"I was thinking about using this lady, Phyllis Pryor. Do you know her?"

"Pryor?" Daddy-O thought about it and shook his head.

"Her last name used to be Olsen or Styles."

"Oh, yeah, I know Phyllis Olsen. She used to be a prosecutor. A damn good one too. Say her name's Pryor now?"

"Yeah, I'm cool with her brother."

"She's good. You can't go wrong with her. Once Phyllis is on the case you might not even get past the preliminaries."

"What is that?"

"That's when the prosecution proves that they have enough evidence to move the case forward.

"Phyllis *will* get to the bottom of this. Be honest with her. That's the only way she can help you," Daddy-O said as he stood up and stretched. "I haven't been up this late in I don't know how long. You hungry?"

"No, I'm tired, but I appreciate you checking on me."

"You're my boy. How is my baby girl doing?"

"She's fine. Oh," Dallas said, remembering the incident with Mrs. Gibson. "If her grandmother ever tries to pick her up again, don't let her."

"Say no more. I told Mattie that lady was a few lightbulbs short of a chandelier."

Dallas nodded his head in agreement.

"Dallas, I know this may seem like a trip through hell, but stay the course. There is a lesson in this. I don't know what it is right now but you can best believe God doesn't put His soldiers through any foolishness for no good reason," Daddy-O said as he reached out and shook Dallas's hand before walking down the steps toward his own house.

"Daddy-O," Dallas called out. "Thanks."

"You're my boy," Daddy-O said as he waved a hand over his head and walked out the gate, casually strolling across the street and up his walkway.

NASTY MAN

For the first time in a long time, Carmen was happy. Once she got the news, she couldn't wait to share it with Sterling. She left work early. She had been waiting for this day all of her life, and now that it was here, she couldn't get home fast enough. She pulled into her garage and almost hit the wall of the house before slamming on the brakes.

"Sterling!" Carmen called out as she rushed into her home. There was no answer. She headed toward the stairs and paused. She thought she heard something. She started climbing the stairs and stopped. Why was her bedroom door closed? Her woman's intuition kicked into overdrive.

Careful not to make any noise, Carmen eased up the rest of the staircase. The closer she got to their bedroom the more clearly she could hear a woman's voice. Her worst nightmare was coming true right in her own house. Suddenly, the best day of her life was quickly deteriorating into the worst. She swallowed the fear that was threatening to overwhelm her.

The woman said something to Sterling. Carmen couldn't hear what it was, but from the woman's tone she knew it was sexual. Then she heard Sterling moan and had to brace herself against a wall. How could this happen? Some heifer was having sex with her husband in her bedroom. She moved toward the door but halted when she heard what was coming out of the mouth of the home wrecker inside.

"Fuck me, fuck me harder!" she screamed. "Oh yeah, give it to me, baby! Harder!"

"Ohhhh. Awwww!" Sterling groaned.

"Oh yeah, baby that's it! Harder, damn it! I'm not your damn wife! Treat me like the whore I am!"

Carmen couldn't believe what she just heard.

What kind of sorry excuse for a man did I marry? she asked herself. How could he stoop so low as to bring another woman into their home? Into their bedroom? She looked down and noticed her hands shaking uncontrollably. She quickly grabbed one hand with the other and forced herself to remain calm.

Carmen closed her eyes and took a few deep breaths to compose herself. She opened her eyes and took a few slow methodical steps toward the bedroom door. Anger was winning out. Now this fool was about to see her other side. The side that she never wanted to ever see again. The side that cut a man's face with a straight razor for trying to molest her when she was thirteen. The side that was born and bred in Carver Homes.

She relaxed her hands because she knew in a matter of seconds she would be scratching and clawing at Sterling's eyes. Then she would deal with the self-proclaimed "whore" on the other side of the door and teach her never to lay her funky little butt on another woman's 1,000-thread count sheets. Her pace quickened in her haste to whip a little butt, but she abruptly stopped when she realized that if she did what her mind was telling her to do, her last image of her husband would be in a compromising position with another woman. Maybe she should take the high road and just ask him to pack up his raggedy behind and leave. After all, she wasn't the same wild thirteen-year-old anymore. She was a well-respected physician. Carmen leaned against the wall to gather herself. It was then that she noticed the vulgar sex talk and moaning on the other side of the door had come to a screeching halt. With the exception of her heavy breathing, the house was eerily silent. Carmen's mind gave the woman a face and visualized her wrapped in Sterling's arms as they comforted each other after a rough round in her bed. On her 1,000-thread count sheets. Oh, hell no. Carmen pulled herself off the wall and rushed toward the bedroom door and kicked it in with all of her might. The door flew open and the first thing she saw was Sterling sitting on the bench at the end of the bed with his boxers down by his knees. He looked like a deer caught in the headlights as he struggled to his feet. Carmen scanned the room for the woman.

"Where is she?" Carmen said, storming into the room. She walked over to the closet and threw open the door. Still no sign of the hoochie with the nasty mouth.

"I said, where is she?"

Sterling looked pale and his eyes were wide. His mouth kept opening and closing as he attempted to speak.

Carmen stomped into the bathroom and looked around. She even opened the cabinets under the sinks and inspected them before walking back into the bedroom to face Sterling. By now he had pulled up his underwear.

"Sterling, where is that woman?" she said, barely controlling her rage.

"Carmen, calm down," Sterling said, reaching out for her.

"You calm down," Carmen said, slapping his hands away. Then she remembered her favorite hiding spot when she was a little girl. Under the bed. She dropped down to her knees and peered under the bed. Nothing!

"I know I'm not crazy," she said, standing up. Her eyes made their way down to her husband's crotch and noticed a liquid dripping down his leg. She turned her attention to the television and noticed a paused shot of a raunchy pornographic movie on the screen. She looked back at Sterling, then to the screen.

"You were in here masturbating?" she asked incredulously.

Sterling looked away and shook his head.

Slowly Carmen put the pieces together. Her relief gave way to laughter.

"I don't see what's so funny," Sterling said with a serious face.

Carmen couldn't stop laughing. She didn't know if she was happier that she hadn't caught her husband cheating or because she had been spared an assault case. Either way, her day was reclaiming its glory.

Sterling sucked his teeth and walked into the bathroom and closed the door. When he returned with only a towel wrapped around him, Carmen had stopped laughing and was lying on the bed naked as a newborn.

"Come on, baby, treat me like a porno star," she said in a seductive voice.

Sterling paused. He had never heard his wife speak this way.

"Carmen, what are you doing?"

"Can't you see?" Carmen said, running her hands across her body, starting at her breasts and working her way down. She had long ago gotten over being ashamed of her large frame. "What are you waiting on?" she asked, closing her eyes.

Sterling felt his manhood growing. He had never seen his wife this sexual and it turned him on.

"I guess I better follow the good doctor's orders," he said, walking over to the bed and crawling onto his wife. Carmen took control, rolling him over onto his back. She eased down onto his chest and ran her tongue over his nipples, tracing up to his neck where she took small bites.

Sterling moaned. Carmen stuck her finger in his mouth, massaging his hard penis with the other hand. She kissed her way down to his manhood and took him into her mouth. Slowly, her head eased up and down. Sterling's legs stiffened and his breathing became rapid. Carmen quickened her pace to match his moaning. Then he grabbed her head to stop her but she pushed his hand away.

"Baby, I'm gonna cu—" he moaned.

"Uh huh," she groaned, not missing a stroke.

Sterling couldn't take it anymore so he pulled Carmen up until she was lying on his chest and their eyes met. Carmen straddled him and slid him into her and began a slow grind. She slid her tongue into his mouth and rode him like her life depended on it.

"Ohhhh, baby," Carmen said, tensing up. She dug her nails into his shoulders before collapsing.

They lay in each other's arms until their breathing returned to normal.

"Baby, that was good," Sterling said with a sly smile.

"Whew," Carmen said, wiping her sweaty hair from her eyes. "Yes, it was."

"Baby," Sterling said. "I have some good news and some bad news."

"Wait, let's save the bad news for tomorrow. I have something to tell you too."

The doorbell rang.

"Are you expecting anyone?" Carmen asked.

"No," Sterling said, jumping up from the bed and looking out of the window. There was a white Lincoln Town Car in the driveway.

"I'll be right back," he said, throwing on some shorts.

Sterling walked down the steps and answered the door.

"Sterling, just the man I wanted to see," Lincoln said.

His bookie had just walked into his house.

SEX BIZ 101

"Block 'em out; act like you in your room by yourself,"
Kitty had told Kameka before she walked on shaky legs
toward the stage for her first solo number.

Kameka stood in the middle of the stage, waiting for
Carl Thomas's soulful voice to fill the room. Once the
music started she swayed seductively to the rhythm. She
closed her eyes and distracted herself by thinking about
her mother. Why did she flip out on her like that? Why
didn't she ever want anything else for herself? Kameka
knew she wanted more than what Carver Homes had to
offer. She dreamed about how her life would turn out
once she made it to college, any college. As she danced,
she only opened her eyes to check her position on the
stage. Once she was secure, her lids closed again. This
time she thought about that trifling Bruce crawling into
her bed and how she'd squeezed his testicles until he'd

damn near passed out. But she'd gained no confidence from the small victory; she still felt vulnerable. That's why she had been so happy to stay with Carmen, but then she overheard Sterling telling someone on the phone that they had "some little ghetto brat" staying at their home. That's when she knew her aunt Carmen's house was no longer a candidate for a home. Hurt was too weak a word to describe how she'd been feeling over the last few weeks.

The music stopped and when Kameka opened her eyes, wads of money lay before her on the stage.

A song by Nelly came on and she moved as if she were in a club dancing with the high school sweetheart she dreamed about. She moved her body to the rhythm, gyrating her hips and slowly making her way to the edge of the stage so that the horny fools could slide their money into her garter. Tips came with ease from all kinds, men, women, young and old. The song ended and she scooped up the cash and raced off the stage. Finally it was over. Now all she had to do was get dressed and go home. That's when it hit her. She had no home. All she had was a spot on Kitty's dirty floor. A tear made its way down her cheek as she made her way off the stage.

"Congratulations," Kitty said, standing at the back of the stage to meet Kameka. "Looks like you made a grip. But I wanna holla at you about making some real money. Not that chump change you just made."

"What?" Kameka answered, wiping her eyes before Kitty could see her condition.

"You're the one. The owner loves you. And the best news is that you were requested."

"What do you mean, requested?" Kameka asked, not really liking where this was going.

"Girl, I'll be glad when you come outta that naïve shit. Now, if it's money you want then you better get your mind right. The *man* wants to see you."

"Who is the man?"

"He was the old man you were dancing for before you went up on stage."

Kameka cringed. *Not that dirty old pervert,* she thought.

Kitty read her expression and went into pimp mode.

"Listen, baby girl." Kitty looked around the corner as if she were about to drop a secret of the pimp game. "You have to use these tricks, and Mr. Batson is the biggest trick of all. Now, didn't I tell you that I would take care of you?"

"That's what you said."

"Well, trust me. I'm not going to put you no place I wouldn't go myself, and believe you me, I loves me. Now, this old dude wanna spend some time with you. It's an easy gig."

"I don't know," Kameka said, uneasy.

"Okay, let me put you up on something. All his old ass wants is some company. Now, if you wanna suck his little shriveled-up-ass dick and make even more money then by all means, do your thing. But you can count on at least a G just to lay down beside him."

Kameka had to stop herself from throwing up when she visualized putting *anybody's* penis in her mouth, never mind the old man's.

"Think about the end result, which are some fat pockets," Kitty said. "Plus, he's a good dude. He don't mean nobody no harm. Just a lonely old man."

Kameka walked away without a response. She looked around at all of the people in the club who were drinking, smoking, and just having a jolly old time. The scene made her want to scream, but instead she kept her head down and went to the back room to count her money.

"Hey, sexy," the old man Kitty had mentioned said as he sidled up behind her, seeming to appear out of nowhere. "Looks like you did well for yourself tonight."

Kameka looked at his reflection in her mirror and nodded her head.

"You wanna get out of here?"

"No, thank you." Kameka smiled politely, hoping he would leave her alone.

"My name is Ringo Batson of Batson Properties. Now, I've had you dance for me all night and what have you made? Five, six hundred dollars?"

"Seven," Kameka said, counting the last of her money and putting it in her purse.

"Well, that's chump change. I wanna offer you something more. A position with my company, making some real money."

"And what do I have to do for this 'position' in your company?"

"Look here, I'm an old man and Viagra don't work too well but I'll tell you what works," the old man said, stepping close to Kameka. He slid his hand over her perky breast and whispered "You" in her ear.

Kameka calmly moved the man's hand and wagged her finger at him as if she were an old pro. She stood up and walked over to her locker.

"Okay, but spend the night with me. We don't have to do anything you don't wanna do. I'll settle for your company. Just wanna feel your soft skin when I wake up," Mr. Batson begged.

"Um-huh," Kameka said, maneuvering her combination lock. "You have a nice night, Mr. Batson."

"Ringo," he said. "Call me Ringo. Hey, listen, I'll pay you two thousand dollars for your time. It's already four o'clock in the morning." The old man looked at his watch. "I mean, how can you turn that down? Four hours for two thousand dollars."

Kameka looked at the old man and thought hard about his offer. Two thousand dollars was more money than she had ever seen in her entire life. Add that to the seven hundred she'd already made, subtract Kitty's fee, and she was still sitting pretty. Plus she wouldn't be sleeping on the floor along with Kitty's other flunkies.

"Let me think about it," she said, but she had pretty much made up her mind. It was a done deal.

"Here," the man said, handing Kameka a wad of bills. "That's just to let you know I'm all about business."

"Let me get dressed. I'll meet you in front of the club," she said.

Mr. Batson smiled and headed out to the parking lot.

STILL A NIGGA

*D*allas rolled over and looked at the clock. 6:00 A.M. He sat up and eased his legs over the edge of the bed. He looked back at his daughter, who was sleeping with her head at the foot of the bed. He shook his head and chuckled.

Girl, you sleep wild just like your mother used to, he thought.

Dallas stood and trudged into the bathroom to take care of his morning basics. He decided he'd take his principal up on her offer and take a few days off. He heard the newspaper hit the ground and he headed downstairs to get it.

"Good morning," he said to Daddy-O, who could always be found, come rain, sleet, or snow, sitting on his front porch reading or just enjoying the break of dawn.

"How you doing?" Daddy-O said, standing and walking over to Dallas's yard. "You get any sleep?"

"Not much. Tossed and turned for a few hours."

"Well, I guess that's to be expected, but you have to get your rest. You're going to need all of your energy for this," he said, showing Dallas the front page of the *Atlanta Journal-Constitution*.

Dallas grabbed the paper and saw a picture of him sitting in the back of a police car under the caption TEACHER OR RAPIST?

"What the hell . . . ?" Dallas said, dropping his own paper and reading Daddy-O's.

He fumbled with the paper and read the first few paragraphs. Lies. All lies.

"Is this legal?" he asked Daddy-O.

"Well, yes. The journalist who wrote the story covered herself by stating the story in question format."

"This is ridiculous. Some people aren't happy unless they can bring a brother down."

"We live in a negative society, Dallas. And unfortunately your misfortune is their entertainment."

"But why the rush to judgment?"

"It seems that what you have here is a journalist trying to make a name for herself."

"Yeah, but it's like she's trying her best to convict me with her words alone. Listen to this: 'Dallas Dupree, a charming and popular teacher who is also a community activist, just may be a sexual predator. Does he prey on unsuspecting women? Does he seduce them with his celebrity? The victim, a twenty-three-year-old substitute teacher, was obviously enamored with him. It has been reported that she took him up on an offer to go to dinner; it was a mistake that would cost her dearly.'

"I asked her out? Whatever happened to responsible reporting?" Dallas yelled. "Whatever happened to doing some damn research? And shouldn't it read 'alleged' victim? I want a front-page apology. Check this out," Dallas said, reading more. "'The dinner took place at Café Intermezzo. Receipts show that Dupree had eight shots of tequila and the victim only ordered water.' Water! 'Her quest for purity would soon end.'" Dallas shook his head. "That girl was about as pure as a swamp."

Daddy-O shook his head. He felt his young neighbor's pain.

"Dallas, let's not worry about the small stuff. The papers are just someone else's opinions. Most journalists don't *do* anything, they make their living writing or reporting about what other people do. And most of the time they can't even do that right. Focus on the big picture."

"You're right. Eight o'clock can't get here soon enough."

"What happens at eight?"

"I'm calling that lawyer."

"Call now. Someone will probably be in the office. When I was practicing, I was there at five o'clock every morning."

Dallas handed the paper back to Daddy-O.

"Okay, I'll talk to you later."

"Keep me posted."

"I will," Dallas said, walking back into his house and straight to the telephone. He sat at the kitchen table and dialed the number to the law offices of Pryor, Capers and Charles. He thought he would at least leave a message, but just like Daddy-O said, someone was there and picked up on the second ring.

"Law offices," the high-pitched babylike voice said.

"Hello, may I speak to Phyllis Pryor, please?"

"She is not in. May I take a message?"

Dallas sighed.

"Hello?" the lady said.

"Yeah, will you ask her to give me a call the minute she walks in? My name is Dallas Dupree and my number is . . ."

"Oh yeah, Mr. Dupree. I was just reading about you."

"It's a lie. All lies, and when this is all over, I want a front-page apology from that newspaper."

"I was talking about an e-mail that Mrs. Pryor sent to me."

Genesis didn't waste any time. I owe him for that, Dallas thought.

"My name is Yolanda Ross and I'll be handling your case. You're her younger brother's friend, right?"

"Yeah," Dallas said, relieved that her perception of him hadn't been tainted by that misinformed man-hating journalist employed by the *Constitution.*

Dallas rubbed his head. He couldn't get over her high-pitched voice.

"Okay, would you like to tell me what happened?" Yolanda asked.

"I don't know what happened."

"Do you know the person's name?"

"Kenya Greer."

"And what are the police charging you with?"

"Sexual assault."

"Do you know if Ms. Greer has contacted anyone?"

"No, but it's all over the paper so somebody told somebody something. How long have you been practicing law?" Dallas blurted out to the babyish-sounding attorney.

"This is my second year. This will be my fourth case."

"Fourth!" Dallas almost screamed. "You know what? Thanks, but no thanks."

"Wait a second. Mr. Dupree, I can assure you that I'm more than qualified to defend you. Mrs. Pryor wouldn't have given me the case if she thought otherwise. I wouldn't even be in this firm."

Dallas contemplated what he had just heard.

"Do you believe in the justice system?" Dallas asked.

"It has its problems, but if you look at other countries, it's the best in the world."

"Well, at this point I'm not concerned about other countries. I'm here and I have no faith in our system. So whomever I choose to represent me, I'm going to have to have faith in them. Out of your three cases, how many of them have you won?"

"All of them," Yolanda said matter-of-factly. She wasn't bragging but simply answering his question.

"You know, I appreciate you agreeing to work on this case but I need a seasoned veteran. This is not a mere case of 'he said, she said.' I'm a black man, and in this society that makes me public enemy number one. And even though I'm innocent, I'm still a nigga, and they would rather have me behind bars than in front of a classroom. Why? Because I help little black boys become men and little black girls become responsible ladies. So, to the powers that be, I'm a threat to their livelihoods because when I teach children how to make intellectually sound decisions, that keeps them from making bad choices and out of those bastards' moneymaking prisons. So you can best believe they would love to lock me up and throw away the key. Innocent or not. They will take me, or any other brother who gives a damn, any way they can get us," Dallas said. "So you see, it's not about my innocence; it's bigger than that."

Yolanda took a deep breath. She had read about Dallas and his good deeds in the paper and was impressed. He was a local celebrity, not for shooting a basketball, running a football, or rapping, but for his mind and his heart.

"You can count on me. I'm up to the task," she said with confidence.

"One mistake and I'm moving on," Dallas said.

"I understand," she said. "And, Dallas . . . I don't know you personally, but in some sort of way I've claimed you as one of the good ones. Our community needs brothers like you and I plan to do everything in my power to make sure we keep you."

"I appreciate you saying that. Now the ball is in your court. And for the record, I'm not capable of harming anyone who doesn't pose a threat to me or my family. These are some bogus charges by a woman who wanted me to be her man and when it didn't work out the way she thought it should, she lied on me."

"Did the police take you in for an exam?"

"Yeah, they took some blood and hair. Look, I'm not saying I didn't have sex with her, although I don't really remember if I did or not."

"Wait a minute. What do you mean you don't remember?"

"I passed out. I had too much to drink and I passed out."

"Humm," Yolanda said, and Dallas could tell she was writing. "Now, what time do you think you can come in to my office today?"

"As soon as I get my daughter dressed."

"So, can I jot you down for eight?"

"That sounds good."

"See you then. And Dallas?"

"Yeah?"

"You're in good hands. I promise."

"God knows I hope so."

ALL TIED UP

*C*armen lay on her back, basking in the afterglow of good sex. It had been awhile since she'd shared a moment like this with her husband, and oh how she missed it. She shook her head and smiled at how angry she had been with him just thirty minutes ago. She rolled over and onto her stomach and slid her hand down between her legs. One orgasm was usually never enough for her, but that was all Sterling seemed to be capable of delivering.

She heard voices downstairs and wondered who Sterling could be talking to at nine o'clock in the morning. Then a tall white man appeared in her doorway. She yanked the bedsheets over her.

"Who are you? And what are you doing in my bedroom?" Carmen said, frantically trying to cover herself.

"Relax, big stuff, it ain't that kind of party," he said, walking over to her bedside and snatching the phone line out of the wall.

"Who are you? Where is my husband?"

"Do you have a cell phone?" the man asked, ignoring Carmen's questions.

"What do you want?" Carmen screamed.

"You better shut up, lady," he commanded sternly.

Carmen did as she was told. Tears sprang to her eyes.

The man looked around the room and found Carmen's purse. He picked it up and peered inside. He tossed the contents on the bed and grabbed her wallet and cell phone. He opened the wallet and took out the money—forty-five dollars. He tossed the money back onto the bed.

"The credit card generation, huh?" he said, shaking his head. "Get dressed."

Carmen didn't move.

"Lady, I've seen more pussy than I care to remember but I've yet to see one I wanted so bad I had to take it." He walked over to her closet and grabbed a pair of jeans and a sweatshirt from the shelves and tossed them to her. "Get dressed under the covers if it'll make you feel better."

"Why are you here?" Carmen asked, trying to keep it together.

"Your husband owes my boss forty thousand dollars."

"What?"

"That's right. Sorry to break the news to you, honey, but your husband is a loser. What did he tell you he did for a living?"

"He's a financial analyst," Carmen said cautiously. She wasn't sure of anything anymore.

The man started laughing and shaking his head as if to say, You dumb bitch. "If Sterling is a financial analyst then I'm Mahatma Gandhi's oldest son. He and money don't get along too well."

Carmen pulled on her clothes under the covers and tossed the covers from the bed. She stood and her hands started shaking again.

"Go on downstairs. Your husband is waiting for you in the kitchen."

Carmen walked down the stairs, and when she saw Sterling it took all of her willpower not to pass out. He was duct taped to the kitchen chair and he appeared to be unconscious. Both of his eyes were red and puffy. Blood trickled from his nose and lips, and two huge men, who were obviously responsible for the assault, stood on either side of him.

"I'll get you the money, just please don't hurt him," Carmen begged.

"I know you will, but Sterling has been a pain in the ass. I don't like getting the runaround for my money," a slim young man said as he removed a cell phone from his hip. "Call whoever you need to call, but don't try any funny business, because I really don't have a problem killing you or this piece of crap." He kicked Sterling's leg like he was a used car tire. Sterling didn't move. "I'm giving you two hours to come up with my money."

Carmen thought back to what Priest tried to tell her. It started to come together. Bruce. The phone call from Sterling's brother. She was confused, but at that moment, Carmen hated Sterling for doing this to their family and for putting her in the position of having to see him like this. It was too much.

"Tell me the number and I'll dial," the man said. "And who are you calling?"

"My brother," Carmen said, rattling off Priest's phone number. The man dialed and handed her the cell phone.

He answered on the first ring.

"Priest, I need for you to listen to me. There are some men here in my home. Sterling owes them forty thousand dollars and they said they are going to kill him if he doesn't pay," Carmen cried.

"Well, I guess you're seeing what I—Anyway . . ." Priest stopped himself, realizing that now was not the time for a lecture.

"They are only giving us two hours to come up with the money," Carmen said, crying hard now. "They said they're going to kill him."

"Did you call the police?"

The tall white man snatched the phone from Carmen. "No, she didn't call the police, and you better not either. If you ever want to see your sister alive again, you'll get that money over here without notifying the police."

"Calm down, brah, I got you. My sister lives almost an hour from me and my bank is an hour in the other direction."

"TMI and NMFP! Too much information and not my fucking problem."

"I was just telling you because I'm coming with the money but I'm going to need a little more time."

"No. Sterling has put us off long enough. Two hours or they both go on a long vacation."

"Wait a minute; Sterling is the one who owes you the money. Take his ass and leave my sister out of this."

"Sterling isn't worth a damn dime dead or alive, never mind forty large. He's a loser. Always has been and always will be. But I see that he's married well, so his debt is now her debt. You know the saying, 'for better or for worse.' Well, it's going to get worse if I don't get my money. Now, you're wasting valuable time," the man said before punching the END key on the cell phone.

PRIEST JUMPED up from the bed and threw on his clothes. He hurried to his study and pulled the carpet back beneath his desk. A silver floor safe automatically rose up. He turned the knobs a few times and the safe clicked open. He removed forty thousand dollars in cash and closed it. The safe disappeared into the floor. He replaced the carpet and left the room. He walked back into his room and sat on the side of the bed.

"Mina, this seems to be the week for family drama. Carmen's punk-for-a-husband has a few loan sharks over at her house and they are threatening Carmen."

"Oh no," Mina said, sitting up in the bed. She liked Carmen a lot. "Poor Carmen."

"Poor Carmen, my ass. She just had to marry this fool."

"Well, Priest, you can't blame her for being in love."

"Love? She didn't even know this fool."

"She must've loved him if she stayed with him after you told her about him and his gambling," Mina said.

"I never told her. I didn't want to tell her while we were dealing with Dallas's mess, but now I wish I would've."

"You want me to ride with you?"

"Nah, by the time you find a pair of shoes Carmen could be dead." Priest stood up and walked into the closet to get dressed.

Mina curled her lips and shook her head.

"I'll call you when I'm on my way back," he said after throwing on a jogging suit. He leaned down and kissed the side of her face.

"Be careful," she said.

"Always."

Priest walked outside and jumped into Mina's Porsche. He would need as much speed as possible to get to Carmen. He knew that most loan sharks were harmless but he wouldn't take any chances when it came to his sister.

As he drove he became more agitated with Carmen. He had done everything in his power to convince her not to marry Sterling but she had been so taken with the pretty boy that she hadn't heard a word he'd said. Yet there had been something in his gut that had told him Sterling was shady and now it was confirmed. Once he had his sister out of harm's way, he would deal with Sterling.

Kameka walked into a marble foyer as she entered Batson's mansion, which was in the ritzy Fayetteville section of Atlanta. She had to give it to him; the man was living large. She followed him down a long hallway lined with beautiful paintings and exotic artwork as they headed toward the living room.

"Have a seat," he said, pointing to a wraparound gray suede sofa that sat at least twelve. In the center of the room was an intricately carved coffee table made of ebony wood.

Kameka sank into the butter-soft furniture. There was a fire burning in the stone fireplace; even though it was a warm night, it was chilly inside Batson's mansion. Tall African sculptures made of the same ebony wood as the coffee table stood in each corner of the room.

"Can I get you something to drink?" Mr. Batson purred.

"No," Kameka said quickly, uttering her first word since leaving the club. *You're not drugging me,* she thought.

"You know my wife is dead. So now it's just me and the dogs. As a matter of fact, you're the first woman to spend the night here since she passed on."

Kameka cut her eyes at him. She wasn't interested in his life or his lies and wanted to get this over with.

"I need the rest of my money."

"Sure," Mr. Batson said as he pulled out a huge roll from his front pocket. He counted off a thousand dollars in hundred-dollar bills and handed it to her. "Now, remember, there's plenty more where that came from," he said and waved the stack in front of Kemeka before putting it back into his pocket. "But only if you're a good girl and do what daddy tells you."

"My daddy is dead," Kameka snapped as her stomach churned.

"I'm sorry to hear that," he said. "Well, the bedroom is this way." He motioned for her to tag along.

Kameka reluctantly stood and followed the old guy into a bedroom that rivaled anything she'd seen on *MTV Cribs.* The bed alone, with its huge wooden posts, was something out of this world.

"You can shower if you like," he said, pointing to the bathroom.

He must've been reading her mind, she thought, because a shower was just the thing she was craving. She'd been hit on one too many times by a few lesbian dancers at the club, and she'd opted not to shower in front of them.

Kameka walked into the bathroom, which was about the same size as her entire apartment at Carver Homes, and locked the door behind her. Marble was everywhere—the counters, the floors, and everything else seemed to be glass and chrome. There was a small television inside the mirror over the sink. She closed her eyes and imagined this place was her home and on the other side of the door was her loving husband.

One day, she thought.

Kameka quickly undressed and stepped into the shower. Water hit her from all angles, soothing her and forcing all of her problems away. Even if only for a moment, she was free. Before long the bathroom was steamy as she did her best to wash away the sinfulness of being in a strip club, the stale cigarettes, and alcohol from her body. Kameka felt like she could stay in the shower forever, but her peacefulness was broken when she heard a knock on the door and Mr. Batson's voice. "You gonna stay in there forever?" he whined.

And just like that she was back to reality. She turned the water off and stepped out onto the cold floor. Mr. Batson had picked the lock and was standing in the doorway naked, his private parts looking like an old prune. Kameka frowned. In her limited world of sex, she had to admit Mr. Batson had the ugliest thing she'd ever seen. He had a crazed look in his eyes and Kameka didn't like what she saw. It was the same lustful gaze that Bruce had worn before he'd tried to force his way into her bed.

Kameka stepped back and tried to cover herself.

"Do you mind?" she said.

Mr. Batson backed out of the room without a word, but his eyes almost paralyzed her.

Kameka started to reconsider what she was about to do but then remembered she didn't have a ride home. She wanted to kick herself for agreeing to come to this man's house. She took her time drying off, lotioned her skin, slid on a fresh set of undies and the same warm-up pants she'd worn earlier, before walking out into the bedroom.

"You can come up outta those pants. I'm paying you to sleep naked."

"You didn't say that. All you said was you wanted my company," Kameka said. She knew what he wanted, but decided to take a chance.

"Hell, I can get anybody to sleep with me, I'm rich. I went to the club to see some ass and that's what I paid for. Now come up outta them clothes and get your little ass in this bed," he barked.

Kameka frowned and removed her clothing. A deal was a deal.

"Whew, shit, now that's what I'm talking about." Mr. Batson whistled, sliding the covers back as he lusted after Kameka's firm teenage curves. "Get on in here, girl."

Kameka slid into the bed and immediately turned her back to Mr. Batson. *This is the last time I'll ever do something like this,* she swore to herself.

"Now, don't be like that," Batson said, easing up behind her and rubbing her shoulder softly. "Slide a little closer to daddy."

"I told you my daddy is dead," Kameka said, gritting her teeth and jumping up from the bed, thoroughly disgusted. "I wanna go home. You can have your money back."

"No, no, no," Mr. Batson said, getting up too. "I'm sorry. I—I—I didn't mean to upset you. Just lie down and get you some rest. Come on now, you've been on your feet all night. My hands will stay on my side of the bed. I promise."

Kameka took a deep breath and stared at the old man. She knew he wasn't going to take her home and she didn't want to see what lengths he'd go to to keep her there, so she eased back into the bed and inched as close to the edge as possible without falling off. As long as he kept his hands to himself, they would be fine. Mr. Batson kept his distance. She forced herself to stay awake but her eyelids were getting heavy. Then she heard a light snore coming from the other side of the bed and the z monster took over.

* * *

KAMEKA WOKE UP to Mr. Batson standing over her. She tried to move her hands but she couldn't pull them down from over her head. She looked up and noticed they were tied to the bedpost.

"What are you doing?" she screamed.

Mr. Batson's eyes were closed tight and he appeared to be straining.

"Get away from me," Kameka yelled at the top of her lungs.

"Nah, you one of them uppity project bitches, huh? You think you can talk to a man like me with disrespect? Well, I got something that'll calm your little ass down and let you know your place."

Kameka realized what he was about to do. He was trying to urinate on her. She instinctively kicked her leg up, catching Mr. Batson in his testicles. He fell down beside her, screaming in pain.

"You little whore," he moaned, holding his family jewels. "I'mma kill you."

Kameka tried to pull her hands free but they were tied too tight. She rolled over and kneed Mr. Batson until he slid away onto the floor. Kameka twisted her body around until her feet were on the outsides of her hands and kicked the headboard until she felt the rope give way. She worked her hands free and jumped right on Mr. Batson, who was still on the floor. She punched and clawed at his eyes.

"You wanna pee on me?" she said, balling her fist and punching him in the back of his head. "You're a sick bastard." Kameka stood and kicked Mr. Batson with all of her might. "That's just plain old nasty."

"Wait, baby," Mr. Batson yelled, trying to cover as much of himself as he could with one hand while the other protected his private parts.

"Nah, you wait," she said, looking around the room. A shoe caught her eye. She grabbed it, flipped it around, and continued beating him with the heel. Batson crawled under the bed to avoid her assault. Kameka stood and quickly grabbed her clothes and bag. She noticed Mr. Batson's pants and snatched them too, before running from the room.

She ran out of the room and into the foyer. She threw on her clothes, grabbed the set of keys Mr. Batson had thrown on a table when they entered, and headed out the same way she came in.

Kameka fumbled around with the keys until they were in the ignition. She had only driven a car once and that was when her uncle Priest had dropped by and let her drive to the store. But now she had no choice if she wanted to get away. She turned the key, put the car in reverse, and slammed on the gas.

Nothing happened.

Damn!

She pounded her fist on the steering wheel. Then she realized the car wasn't on. She put the car in park and turned the key all the way. The engine roared to life. She tried reverse again and once again slammed on the gas pedal. There was a huge crash as she backed the car through the garage door but she wasn't stopping; she kept going until she was on the street on front of the house. Kameka pulled the gear shift into the drive position and the car lurched forward. She weaved all over the road as she pressed the gas pedal to the floor. Kameka drove until she was at the end of the street and hit the brakes when she came to the huge gate they had entered earlier. She turned the wheel toward the gate and noticed a car waiting for it to open, but she didn't have that kind of time. There was an old freak back at the house who wanted to pee on her. She slammed through the gate, knocking one of the sides off of its hinges, and turned right. She kept going until she came to a dead end. She cursed again and wished she had paid more attention to the way she had come in. She backed up and headed down another street, where she saw a blue-and-red sign that read 85N. Bingo. She tried to keep the car steady as she took to the highway.

Kameka passed a police officer. He looked at her. She kept her eyes straight and acted like she was bobbing her head to some music. His lights came on. Her heart raced as she prepared to tell the man exactly what had happened to her. She got over in the far right lane but the officer sped past her. She was free to continue her getaway in the high-priced luxury car. She got off on the Auburn Avenue exit and pulled the car over in front of a statue of Martin Luther King Jr. She put the car in park and grabbed her bags. Kameka picked up Mr. Batson's pants, went through the pockets, removed the same huge roll of money that he'd tempted her with last night, and used the pants to wipe away her fingerprints from the steering wheel and gear shift. Once she was satisfied that any signs of her had been removed from the vehicle, she got out, walked across the street to the bus stop, and took a seat.

Her nightmare was over. Well, not exactly. She noticed a pink Cadillac heading her way. Kitty.

"Girl, what the hell happened to you?" Kitty asked.

Kameka narrowed her eyes but remained silent.

"Come on, Sade, talk to me," Kitty said from inside the car.

"My name ain't Sade! And how did you find me this quick?"

"You think I send my girls out on dates without escorts? I had one of my boys posted outside the gates to keep an eye on you. Then he called to tell me you were weaving all over the damn road and I jumped up and came over. Get in."

"I'm okay," Kameka said, looking at her fingernails.

"Whatchu mean you okay?"

"I'm done with that business. Forget I ever came to you."

"That's cool, but you still owe me some money."

"How much do I owe you?"

"How much did you make?"

"Ten dollars," Kameka said sarcastically.

"Now, we can handle this easy or hard," Kitty said, opening the glove compartment and removing a gun. "How you wanna handle it?"

"You wanna shoot me?" Kameka said, standing up and shouting. She could afford to be bold since it was a little after nine in the morning and the streets were crowded with people getting to work.

Kitty looked around and thought better of the gun thing. She put it back.

"So, it's like that?" Kitty said. "I take you in when your own momma and your uppity-ass aunt didn't want you, and this is how you act?"

"And I asked you, how much do I owe you?"

"I work on commission. It's all about how much you make."

"I didn't get my money from that old dude. He tried to pee on me so I left."

"You know he called the police on you."

Kameka's heart picked up its pace. She had never thought about going to jail.

"But I got your back. Now, if you come correct, I'll say you were with me all night and it'll be his word against ours, but I need my cheddar."

Kameka opened her bag and removed the money Mr. Batson had handed her in the club. It was a thousand dollars. She peeled off five hundred-dollar bills and threw them into the car at Kitty.

"Now you happy? You got half of what I got."

"Fine with me, but don't bring your li'l ass 'round me no more wanting me to save you."

Kameka sat back down and folded her arms as Kitty's pink Cadillac drove down the street. She went through her bag and removed a tablet with her phone numbers on it. She called her uncle Dallas.

THE KILLING MOOD

*P*riest parked two streets over from his sister's house and figured out his plan of attack. He removed his Glock semi-automatic from under the seat and cocked a round into the chamber. He stepped from the car, walking between houses until he came to Carmen's backyard. A brick wall separated her property from her neighbor's, and Priest walked to the corner of her yard and tried to see into her place. He couldn't see anyone through the kitchen window so he vaulted over the wall and crept up to the back door. He peered through the window and saw Sterling sitting in a chair flanked by two guys in black suits. What a pathetic sight, Priest thought. He was tempted to point his pistol through the window and let off a few rounds at his low-down brother-in-law, but he held back. Sterling was who he was, and as far as

Priest was concerned, Carmen should shoulder some of the blame for marrying that buster in the first place.

Priest looked around for a quiet entry into the house. The last thing he wanted to do was set these guys off and have them hurt Carmen. If that was to happen, then he would personally make sure Sterling died a slow and agonizing death. He eased around to the front of the house. If these guys were true pros they would have someone posted there, but when he peeked around the corner he saw nothing but a car, which looked to be empty. He stayed low, ran to the front door, and jimmied the lock. He removed his chewing gum from his mouth and took a dime from his pocket. He placed the dime on the gum and slipped it over the door sensor alarm so he wouldn't alert the goons inside to the fact that they had company.

Once inside the house, Priest heard Sterling pleading and begging.

Ain't no way I'd let my wife hear me crying like a little bitch, he thought.

Priest shook his head and crept through the living room, making sure he stayed low and close to the walls. He came up to the door and saw Carmen sitting on the floor with her arms around her knees. She was sobbing, and it broke his heart to see her like this. She lifted her head and saw him. Priest quickly placed a finger to his mouth and surveyed the room. The two goons still stood beside Sterling with their arms crossed.

Good sign. Obviously they had watched too many gangster movies and were acting out their parts. If something did jump off, by the time they got their arms down to their weapons it would be too late. There was another man—a big guy—standing by the sink and he kept looking at his watch. This was going to be way too easy, Priest thought. He decided to stop giving these guys the respect they didn't deserve and just walked into the kitchen with his gun pointed at the man by the sink.

"You boys move and it could get real bloody in here," Priest growled.

One of the goons looked like he wanted to run, but the other reached for his gun.

"Go for it," Priest said, pointing his gun at him with a sinister smile. He walked over to the guy and placed the gun to his head.

"Please," the guy begged. "I have a family."

"So?" Priest said.

"Wait a minute," Lincoln said, holding up his hands. "We're not here for any trouble."

"Well, what are you here for?" Priest asked, the gun still at the man's head. "Drop whatever weapons you have on the floor."

The goons did as they were told and dropped two little handguns on the tile.

Priest patted the men down. God, he missed his days on the police force.

"Look," Lincoln said. "I just want my money. I'm a businessman and . . . well, if I wanted to hurt these people, I would have a long time ago."

"Well, now you've lost that opportunity, so leave."

Lincoln looked confused.

"What about my money?"

"What about it?" Priest challenged.

"This man owes me," he said, pointing at Sterling.

"Take him with you. I'm only concerned with her," Priest said, nodding toward Carmen. "Come over here, Carmen," he said to his sister.

She did as she was told and ran behind Priest the same way she did when she was younger and the older kids picked on her.

"Priest, please don't let them hurt him," Carmen pleaded.

Priest sighed and grimaced at Sterling. Sterling's frightened eyes met his gaze. He felt no pity for the man and thought about what he'd do to Sterling if Carmen weren't there.

"Carmen, you can do better than this! After all of the sacrifices you've made to become somebody, you wanna share your life with this sorry piece of crap? You could've stayed in the projects and got a model like this one."

"Priest, please." She tugged his arm.

Priest growled and removed a stack of money from his back pocket with his free hand. He tossed it to Lincoln.

"That's twenty thousand. Consider the debt settled. Now get the fuck out of here."

Lincoln caught the money and rushed to the door without looking back.

Priest looked at the goons and hunched his shoulders as if to ask them what were they waiting on.

"Would you like for us to untie him?" the one with the family offered.

"Nah," Priest said, still pointing the gun at them.

He held the gun on them until they were out of the house and into their car. He watched them as they pulled away. When he walked back into the house Carmen was working on untaping Sterling from the chair.

"Leave him alone," Priest barked. "And give us a minute."

"Thanks, Priest, man . . ." Sterling started to gush.

"Shut up," Priest commanded.

"Priest, please let me handle this," Carmen said.

"Carmen," Priest said, easing his gun into his back holster, "you have been misled and that's okay. We all make mistakes, but don't be a fool. Now that you see what kind of guy he is, it's time to move on."

"But he's still my husband. And like you said, we all make mistakes."

"Carmen, give me a minute with *your husband*."

Carmen looked at Sterling; she was upset with him but she still cared for him. And she knew too well the way Priest felt about him, but too much was going on in her head for her to fight with either of them. She threw up her hands and walked out of the room.

"Now, look here, player," Priest said, walking over to Sterling, "I'm not going to waste a lot of words with you. You just cost me twenty thousand dollars."

"I'll pay you back, man, I promise," Sterling whined.

"Let it go," Priest said. He lowered his tone to just above a whisper. "Now, we both know you can't pay it back. But I'll work out a deal with ya. And you should consider yourself the luckiest man in the world, because I don't make deals. So here's what I propose. You go pack your things, leave the state, and I'll call it a day. But you need to know that if I see you again, I'm going to kill you. No questions asked. I could see you in church with your new family and I'll put a nice silver bullet right there," Priest said, poking Sterling between his eyes. *"Comprende?"*

"I understand," Sterling said.

"I'm going to go and get my car; it's not too far from here. By the time I get back you better be ready to roll. What you can't pack in the next three or four minutes you don't take. Are we clear?"

"I got you, man, but Priest . . . I love Carmen. I just got a little gambling problem."

Priest wasn't willing to hear any sob stories from Sterling.

"Sterling, that's too bad, but you're unworthy of my sister. You think I don't know your game? You find a woman who has it going on financially. Hopefully she has low self-esteem. You come in, make her feel like she's the best thing since sliced bread, then you slither your way into her pockets. Three minutes, and you better thank God that I'm not in the killing mood today or I would be dumping your sorry ass into a river somewhere," Priest said, walking out the back door.

Sterling called out to Carmen, and she ran back into the room.

"Help me get loose, baby," he said.

"What did he say?" Carmen said as she removed the duct tape.

"Baby, I don't have time to explain it to you. I gotta get my things together. Quick," he said, looking at the clock over the stove.

Carmen freed Sterling from the chair and he took off running up the stairs. She ran after him.

"Sterling, what is going on?"

"Baby, I gotta go away for a while," he said, throwing some clothes into a bag. "I'll call you when I get settled."

Carmen took a deep breath and rubbed her arm. This was not the way she wanted this to end, but she had to admit it was time for Sterling to go. She realized that she knew very little about the man she'd married. The man whose baby she was carrying.

"I want you to know that I do love you," he said, still gathering his things. "I'm sorry I put you through that."

Carmen didn't answer. She couldn't. She heard a car pull into the driveway and walked over to the window. She saw Priest get out of the car and walk up to the house.

Sterling closed his bag and walked over to Carmen. He looked into her teary eyes and leaned down to kiss her. She turned her head away. He looked around nervously and walked down the stairs and out the front door without even saying good-bye.

Priest was waiting for him.

"Go and get in the car," he ordered as if Sterling were a child.

Sterling nodded and kept moving.

Priest looked up at the top of the stairs and saw his sister crying. He walked up the steps and took her in his arms.

"Everything's gonna be okay, baby girl."

"Priest," she cried. "I'm pregnant."

Priest looked up. *Why, God?* he thought. *Why this, why now?* "Baby girl, listen." He touched Carmen's face, tilting it up so he could look into her eyes. "You and the baby will be better off without him. Trust me on that," he said before taking his sister back into his arms.

"But I didn't get a chance to tell him about the baby. Don't you think he might change if he knows?"

Priest shook his head. "Baby girl, with men like Sterling, the only thing that changes is the game."

Carmen stared out the window over her foyer. She saw Sterling sitting on the hood of Priest's car as if everything were okay and knew that her brother was right about her *husband*.

ANTOINE

*D*allas picked up the phone and heard his niece's voice. He felt guilty because it had been a long time since they had spoken. Too long. She sounded distressed.

"Uncle Dallas," Kameka said in a shaky voice.

"Hey, sweetie. How are ya?"

"Not too good. Can you come and get me?" she asked.

"Where are you?"

"I'm on the corner of Auburn Avenue by that statue of Martin Luther King," Kameka said. Dallas could barely understand her through her crying.

"You stay put. I'm on my way," Dallas said before hanging up.

As soon as he had a dial tone he called Yolanda Ross.

"Yolanda Ross."

"Ms. Ross, I'm going to have to reschedule our

meeting. My niece just called, so I gotta take care of some family business. Can I call you later and set up a time?"

"Sure, Mr. Dupree, but take my cell number just in case you don't get back to me before three." Yolanda rattled off a cell phone number. "I teach a dance class."

Three? What the hell kind of lawyer works until three o'clock in the afternoon? Dallas still wasn't confident about his attorney and fought off the urge to tell her that he would be seeking new counsel immediately. How could she represent him effectively if she was running around playing Debbie Allen? He needed a lawyer who would devote his or her every waking moment to his case.

"All right," he said slowly as he wrote down the number. He would deal with her later.

"Actually it will work out better if we meet later. That will give me some time to run over to the hospital, pick up the results from your blood test, and call the D.A.'s office," Yolanda said.

Dallas nodded but he still didn't like her. Something didn't seem right about his lawyer leaving work to go dancing.

"Sounds good," he said, hanging up the phone abruptly.

Dallas walked into his bedroom to rouse Aja.

"Good morning, precious," Dallas sang as he walked over to her bed. Whatever else he was going through, his stresses fell away when he was around her. She made everything all right. He knelt down beside her and whispered, "It's time to wake up."

"Good morning, Daddy," Aja said in her husky sleep-filled voice.

Dallas stood and picked her up. He carried her into her bathroom next to her bedroom and stood her in front of the sink.

"Now, brush your teeth and wash your face. I'll lay your clothes out for you."

"Okay," she said, closing the door behind her father.

Dallas walked into Aja's pink-and-white bedroom. With its canopy bed, it was a room fit for a princess. He walked into her closet and shook his head at all of the clothes his little girl had.

"I got this girl spoiled." He chuckled, picking out a pair of khaki shorts and a white polo shirt.

"I'm done," Aja said, walking into her bedroom.

"Let me smell your breath," he said, leaning down as she blew in his face. He frowned and made a face as if he were about to get sick.

"Daddy," she whined. "Stop it."

Dallas smiled and kissed her forehead.

"Okay, precious, get dressed. I'll go and fix something for your breakfast. Hurry up."

Dallas rushed downstairs and into the kitchen, where he grabbed a few beef links and tossed them into the microwave. He popped a waffle in the toaster.

Aja ambled down with her book bag on her back.

"You ready?"

"Yes," she said and she gave him a strange look. "Daddy, are you going to jail today?"

"No," he said, removing the sausage and draining the grease on a towel. "Didn't I tell you that was a mistake? I'm never going to jail. Now, come on."

Dallas put the sausages and the waffle on a plate and handed it to Aja. After she ate they hurried across the street to Mrs. Morton's house.

"Daddy's not going to work today so I might be back to pick you up early, okay?"

"Yaaaay," she said, raising her little arms in the air and smiling from ear to ear.

Mrs. Morton was waiting for them on the porch.

"Good morning, you two."

"Good morning," Dallas and Aja said in unison. "Mrs. Morton, don't let anyone pick her up, okay?" Dallas said.

"You don't have to worry about that. She's in good hands."

"Where is Daddy-O?"

"He went downtown to speak with a group of lawyers. He's on some board. You know, sometimes I wonder if he's really retired or if he just told me that so I'd shut up about him working so hard," she said, laughing at her own joke.

Dallas smiled.

"Well, I gotta run," he said, leaning down and kissing his daughter. "See you guys later. Love ya."

"Love you too, Daddy," Aja said.

"You be careful, Dallas," Mrs. Morton said.

Dallas walked back to his house and hopped into his Lexus. He drove quickly to his niece. Something in her voice troubled him. It didn't take long for him to find Kameka. She was on the corner, pacing back and forth like a caged animal. Even from afar he could see the weight of the world on her shoulders.

Dallas pulled up in front of her and opened the door.

"Hey, Uncle Dallas," she said cautiously as she got into the car.

"Hi, Kameka," Dallas said. "Why aren't you in school?"

Kameka hunched her shoulders but didn't answer.

Dallas changed the subject. He'd been around enough kids to know when to push and when not to. Now was not the time.

"Are you hungry?"

She nodded her head.

"Good. Me too," he said, whipping his car around to get back on the interstate. "Anything in particular you want?"

"McDonald's will do for me," she said.

"Oh, too much of that stuff will kill ya. Let's go somewhere where we can sit down and talk. Is that all right?"

Kameka nodded and Dallas saw her face relax a little. Though he had been lax lately, whenever he did spend time with her, they always had fun together.

Dallas took the Lenox Road exit and headed toward The Palms restaurant in Buckhead. The valet parked his car and he reached for Kameka's hand as they walked into the upscale restaurant.

"You and Aunt Carmen love these fancy places," she said, grabbing her uncle's hand.

"This is my favorite restaurant in the whole wide world," Dallas said with a smile. "And you're my date for the morning."

Kameka shook her head and Dallas thought he saw a smile.

They were seated by a window in the front of the restaurant. The waiter came, filled their glasses with water, and took their order.

"Get whatever you want," Dallas encouraged. "These guys can definitely burn."

"I just want some eggs and bacon," Kameka said, then she quickly added, "oh, and some French toast. Do they have omelets?"

Dallas smiled.

"I guess I'm hungrier than I thought," she said.

"It's all good. Eat till your heart's content."

After they ordered they sat quietly for a few minutes. Then Kameka spoke.

"Uncle Dallas, why didn't y'all spend more time with me?" she said.

Dallas was caught off guard by her question.

"Well, Kameka, I don't really know why. I have no excuses for my part, but sometimes people get caught up in their own little worlds and time just keeps on ticking. And before you know it . . ." He hunched his shoulders.

"I understand, but not coming from you. I mean, I read about you in the paper all the time doing stuff with kids that aren't even your blood."

Dallas nodded.

"I'm sorry, Kameka, but I'll tell you what," he said, reaching for her hand. "If you can forgive me, I promise I'll do much better. You know you're my favorite niece."

"I'm your only niece, Uncle Dallas." She gave a weak laugh. "How is Aja?"

"She's doing good. You wanna see her today? I know she'd love to see you."

"Yeah," Kameka said. "I'd like that."

"Cool."

Dallas looked across the table and Kameka dropped her head. She seemed to be going through some inner turmoil. She started to sob. He stood and walked around the table to comfort his niece.

"Hey," he said, massaging her shoulders. "Everything is fine now."

"I can't do it," she said, shaking her head.

"Can't do what?"

"I can't do it on my own. I thought I could, but I can't."

"What, sweetie?"

"I tried to get my own place, and I can't do it," she said, pulling herself away and trying to contain her tears. Dallas could tell that his niece was not used to having anyone to lean on. He would take the blame for that.

"What happened with Carmen?"

Kameka shook her head from side to side. "Her husband didn't want me there."

"What?"

"I overheard him on the phone one day saying something about me being ghetto and taking all of his wife's time."

Dallas made a mental note to put his foot in Sterling's rear end.

"I'm sorry about that, Kameka. Did you tell Carmen what you heard?"

"No, I know they just got married. So I just left. Didn't want to be in the way."

"Nah, you are family, you are never in the way."

Kameka was silent for what seemed like forever.

"Uncle Dallas, will you tell me how my father died? I mean, I know he got shot, but what happened?"

Dallas took a deep breath and sighed so hard the linen napkin moved. His mind went back to that day, long ago, a day he wished would've never happened. The day that drove him to do his part in saving children.

"Well, I was thirteen and your dad had just turned sixteen. He would come over to the middle school and wait for me every day. Aw, man, he was so cool," Dallas said, lost in his own memories now. "Anyway, this day was no different."

"*HOW WAS your day, Dallas?*" Antoine asked.

"*It was cool. Mrs. Heath gave us all this homework.*"

Antoine smiled. "*She still doing that? Man, she used to give me a ton of homework. By the time I finished I didn't have time to go outside and play,*" *he said, shaking his head.*

The boys walked onto the property of their projects and some skinny guy rode by on his bicycle. "*Y'all momma dead,*" *he said.*

"*What?*" *Antoine said.*

"*She up at Jesse's,*" *the guy said, and rode off.*

Antoine and Dallas kept walking in silence.

"*I should've punched him in his face for playing like that,*" *Antoine said.* "*Dumb crackheads play too much. He probably trynna scare some-body so he can get a laugh.*"

"*Maybe he telling the truth, Twoine,*" *Dallas said.* "*Let's go see.*"

Antoine stopped and looked at Dallas. "My . . . Our mother is not dead. That stupid dude was high as a kite. He's just trynna see us run. So he can get a laugh."

Dallas dropped his book bag and took off running. Antoine picked up his bag and followed his little brother.

They made it to Jesse's, the spot where the drug folks shot their poison, and got the shock of their young lives.

Sara Dupree was lying on the floor with the hypodermic needle still stuck in her arm.

Dallas ran over and knelt down beside their mother. Antoine stood at the door in shock. A few seconds later Priest entered. He wasn't as cool as his younger brothers.

"You motherfuckers," Priest yelled, staring down at his mother's twisted body. "Y'all killed her."

Priest started throwing folks around. Punching any and everyone in sight.

A man who was known as the neighborhood drug dealer stood up and pointed a gun at Priest. Antoine saw what was happening and ran and jumped onto the dealer's back. He wrapped his arms tightly around the man's neck, trying his best to choke the life out of him. The man struggled to breathe and somehow managed to get the gun above his neck.

Bam. The gun exploded.

Antoine released the man. He half smiled at Priest as he walked over to their mother. He rubbed Dallas on his head and casually lay down beside his mother. He was gone. Confused, Priest walked over to Antoine and tried to open his eyes. He turned to the dealer, no longer caring if he lived or died. He ran at the man and before the man could lift his gun again, he was hit like a Mack truck. Priest wrestled the gun from the man's hand and turned it on him. He pulled the trigger.

Click.

Click.

Click. *The gun had jammed.*

"Damn you!" Priest yelled, and threw the gun at the man. Then he commenced to beating him with everything he had until the man was a bloody mess. Priest stood and lifted Antoine.

"Get Momma," he said to Dallas in a cracked voice.

Dallas did as he was told and they took Antoine and their mother home. Priest put them in the bed together and pulled the sheets up around them as if they were just napping.

"WE BURIED our mother and brother on the same day," Dallas said to Kameka.

"I'm sorry, Uncle Dallas," Kameka said, rubbing his hand.

Dallas wiped the corners of his eyes. "Kameka, when things like that happen, people's natural reaction is to try and forget. Maybe you reminded us all of Antoine so much that . . . in our own selfish ways, we let you down. But as of today, we'll move forward. If that's all right with you."

Kameka's eyes filled with tears. She finally had her answer, and to her, her father was a hero. He was her Malcolm X. He died trying to save his brother. In some strange way she felt better knowing he didn't die for nothing. She was proud to have him as a father.

"Uncle Dallas, c-c-can I live with you?" she asked tentatively.

Dallas smiled and said, "You don't even have to ask."

24

*P*riest studied the face of the woman who had falsely accused his brother of sexual assault. He had used up practically all of his favors with the police department to get her picture and a few other goodies. Now that he had a little background on the girl, he contemplated his next move.

Mina entered the house. She had been grocery shopping, and after depositing her bags in the kitchen she plopped down beside him at the kitchen table.

"How was your day?" she asked, leaning over to kiss him.

"Busy," he said, and kissed her back. "What about you?"

"Busy too. I registered for school today," she said with a smile. "I'm going to Georgia State University. And the best part is that most of my classes from home transferred. So I'm only a year away from completing my degree in design."

Priest stopped what he was doing and reached over and pulled her close to him. Mina was such a pleasant woman. He loved her for her strength and resolve. From the moment she opened up to him, she was talking about her clothing ideas and now she was getting back on track to completing her goals.

"I'm proud of you, love," he said. "This is cause for a celebration."

Mina smiled. "Maybe we can celebrate this weekend. I registered late and classes have already begun so I must get ready. I'm a schoolgirl," she said happily as she hurried out of the room.

"Well, you do your thing, baby," Priest said.

"Oh," Mina said returning to the door. "You left your cell phone home and it rang a few times. I put your messages on the counter in the kitchen."

Priest stood and walked into the kitchen. He read the messages as he walked back into the living room.

Carmen called.

Dallas called, said your niece Kameka was now living with him and for you to come by and see her.

Escada called.

Priest tossed the pictures on the table and his mind shifted to his other business.

"When did Escada call?" Priest yelled to Mina.

"About an hour after you left. Who is he?"

"Somebody that I need to talk to," Priest said as he scrolled through the numbers in his cell phone. "This man does million-dollar deals every other week. I've been trying to get close to him for a long time."

"Maybe it's a good thing that you didn't get the call," Mina said cautiously.

Priest gave her a warning look.

"Come on, Priest, we're doing fine. Why do you need to keep upping the ante?"

"Because he's doing big business and it's time I moved to the next level."

"Priest, I've always stayed out of your affairs, but . . ."

Priest put his finger to her lips to keep her from talking. He slowly shook his head, letting her know she had been doing a good job of staying out of his business and not to mess it up now. He stood and walked out of the room.

Mina shook her head. "No, I must say this. I come from nothing and you've given me everything. What I'm trying to say is, I don't want to lose you. Your business is very dangerous," she said quietly. "I'm scared for you. For me. For us."

"Don't be," Priest said. "Once I touch this guy, things will change. You'll see."

Mina threw up her hands in surrender. Just as she was about to walk out, she caught sight of the picture on the table.

"Priest?" she said. "Why do you have a picture of Destiny?"

"Who's Destiny?"

Mina pointed at the picture.

Priest grabbed it.

"You know her?"

"Yeah, she used to work with me back in the day when I was . . . you know," Mina said, not wanting to think about her days on the stroll.

Priest studied the face of the pretty brown woman with the lifeless eyes.

"Are you sure this is the same woman that you knew?"

"Yes," Mina said, taking the photo from Priest and studying it closely. "It's her. She works for Lord."

"This is the lady that accused Dallas of raping her. She's a teacher."

"You're kidding," Mina said, surprised. "Destiny's a teacher?"

"Maybe she moved on to bigger and better things. Dallas said she was a teacher."

"She was smart, but she wasn't right in the head. I think she was bipolar or something like that. She took medication for whatever her problem was."

"Mina, are you sure you have the right woman?" Priest asked again.

"Yes, Priest, I'm sure."

Things were starting to come together for Priest. "Okay. If anyone calls me, give them my cell," Priest said and was out the door.

AFTER DRIVING around for more than two hours asking about the whereabouts of one Kenya Greer, Priest found himself seated in the rear of Mt. Zion Baptist Church enjoying the spectacle before him.

Standing behind the podium was a burly man with sweat running from his bald meaty head onto his shiny hairless face. The preacher, who was dressed more like a pimp than a man of the cloth in his bright green suit, whooped and hollered his version of God's word between chords from the organ player.

"If Gawd said it." *Bruuuummmm*, the organ blared. "Then He'll do it." *Bruuuummmm*. "If He takes you to it." *Bruuuummmm*. "Then He'll bring you through it." *Bruuuummmm*. "Ummm-n-huh."

The assistant pastors offered their perfectly timed "Wells," then a few "Hmmms," and when it really got good one of them stood and fanned a hand as if shooing the preacher away, shouting, "Gone now! You better preach!"

And the congregation joined right in. They stood and jumped around, passing out as if their bodies were being taken over by some invisible spirit. It seemed like they were trying to out-shout one another to get God's attention because their individual problems were the only ones that truly mattered.

From the time he was a little boy, one thing that had always baffled Priest when their mother would drag him and his siblings off to their Sunday-morning blessing sessions, was how, when the music stopped, the spirit that had had these people jumping around so hard just moments before would miraculously leave their bodies and everything would return to normal.

Priest had never been a fan of the organized church or of any one religious denomination. No, he'd seen too many people taken to the cleaners by hustlers disguised as men of God. And he wasn't too fond of hustlers, regardless of where they were. He figured his chances of enjoying the afterlife were better if he depended on his own ability to discern God's words. So he read his Bible and his Koran and tithed by helping those in the streets.

But even Priest couldn't resist the lure of the music. When the choir went into a tune Priest remembered hearing on the radio he stood up and clapped along with the song, much to the delight of those who were watching him—a handsome new prosperous-looking member of the congregation.

The good Reverend Pimp Daddy settled down. He wiped the sweat from his face and motioned for one of the assistant pastors to get him a drink of water. The pastor jumped as if he were serving Jesus Himself. Once his thirst was satisfied, he said it was time for the tithes and offerings. He preached for a full ten minutes about the sins of cheating God.

"Remember, the more you give, the more you'll receive from Gawd," Reverend Pimp Daddy said in his thunderous voice. "Oh, y'all don't hear me. I said the more you bless, the more you'll be blessed. I can tell you, once I reached into my pockets and stopped cheating Gawd, I went from a Hyundai to a Cadillac, from a one-room shack to having a pool out back, from having no money to having mo' money, mo' money, mo' money. Y'all don't hear me. I said I surrendered myself *and* my money to the man upstairs, and whooooo, I'll tell you. My life's been changed."

Priest looked around the congregation and watched as men and women happily reached in pockets and purses to do their part in not cheating God. He felt sorry for them. They were so desperate to believe in something that they trusted anything that resembled a savior.

Before Priest could get too deep into his thoughts, a middle-aged woman came up beside him. She handed him a blue-and-gold bucket the size of a small wastebasket. He looked at it and passed it on down the aisle.

The woman narrowed her eyes at him and snarled as if he were a heathen.

The good reverend told a few more lies, the choir sang a few more songs, a few more people passed out, and then the show was over.

Priest sat until the majority of the parishioners filed out. Most of them stopped to shake his hand. Why? He had no idea. An attractive lady walked over and introduced herself. He shook her hand and before she could find her a good man who was into the church, he excused himself and walked toward the front of the church where the Reverend Pimp Daddy was laying hands on a female member of the congregation. Priest waited patiently for the reverend to finish his free feel.

"I need to see you," Priest said, stopping directly in front of the good reverend.

The Reverend Pimp Daddy looked around nervously. It was as if Lucifer himself had shown up to take him away for the crime of false prophecy. Priest used to arrest him just about every other week for petty crimes when the good pastor was living "in the world."

"Ahh, Detective Dupree, how are you this fine day Gawd has given us?"

"Theofis, follow me," Priest said and walked out of the sanctuary and toward the pastor's office.

Pastor Theofis ignored the other people waiting to have a word with him and followed Priest.

"Sure am surprised to see you here today."

"You really put on a good show."

"I . . . I . . . I do the best I can," Theofis said nervously as he walked into his office and took a seat behind his desk.

"I'll be brief," Priest said. "I'm looking for this girl." He handed Theofis a photo of Kenya.

"Oh, that's Kenyatta. Poor girl. She was recently assaulted. Are you investigating that crime?"

"I'm doing a little PI work. Do you know where I could find her?"

"She's in the back counting money. She works in the treasury. Would you like for me to have her paged?"

"Oh, yeah. I need a word or two with her."

25

READY TO RUMBLE

For the first time since his arrest Dallas didn't feel a sense of dread gripping his stomach. As a matter of fact, he was having a pretty good day. As he sat with his feet propped up watching Kameka smile as she showed Aja how to do her doll baby's hair, his problems seemed a million miles away. His phone rang, and he was tempted not to answer it.

Ever since the arrest, his phone hadn't stopped ringing. Well-wishers and nosy folks alike were on him constantly and although he appreciated the kindness and concern, it got old real quick. He looked at the caller ID, which read ALONZO CRIM HIGH SCHOOL.

"Hello," Dallas said cautiously.

"Mr. Dupree, how you just gonna *not* come to work?" his student D.J. said. "What the problem is?"

"D.J., I don't know what the problem is. Obviously you've been skipping your English class."

"There you go," D.J. said.

"How you doing, man?" Dallas said, happy to hear his student's voice.

"I'm cool. How you doing?"

"Hanging on in there."

"When you coming back to school?"

"Maybe on Monday."

"I don't know if I can hold off from killing one of these busters that long."

"Well, you give it some effort," Dallas instructed. "Now listen, I'm sure you've heard about what's going on with me, but I want you to know it's not true."

"Aw, man, everybody knows that. If you want me to, I'll testify that I saw Ms. Greer trynna sex you up in the lunchroom."

"Boy, you are too much. How is everybody else doing?"

"Everybody straight. Keith's old racist ass still living. And I got a surprise for you."

"A'ight, boy. You better watch your mouth. Just because I'm not there doesn't mean you can act a fool," Dallas chided.

"Speak of the devil. The grand wizard himself just walked in. I'll let him tell you the news."

Dallas heard Keith and D.J. arguing about something, then Keith's country twang came on the line.

"Mr. Dupree. How you holding up?"

"I'm fine, Keith. What about you?"

"Not too good," Keith said. "My daddy kicked me out the house."

"Why did your father kick you out?"

"Cuz he's old-fashion and still is holding on to some twisted ways."

"I'm listening."

"He got a little upset when I defended you. You know they got you all over the news. He said I was becoming a nigger lover and no such animal was living in his house," Keith said.

Dallas heard D.J. in the background, daring Keith to say that word again. "Man, shut up. I was talking to Mr. Dupree," Keith said in his own defense.

"Keith, where are you staying?" Dallas asked.

"In hell."

"Boy, where are you staying?" Dallas said, getting concerned. Keith was a handful but he was his.

"You won't believe it. With D.J., and I'll tell you, ain't no hell like the one I'm in."

Dallas laughed.

"Got me listening to that rap crap first thing in the morning and the last thing at night. He wouldn't let me stay unless I left all of my Clint Black and Garth Brooks CDs at home. I got to keep my Metallica though. You know, they violent so he was okay with that," Keith said. Then his voice went to a whisper. "I still got my Randy Travis though."

"Boy, if y'all gonna act like this I need to take more days off."

"Hold on," Keith said, arguing with someone else in the background. "Jonnea wanna talk to you. You hurry back now, ya hear?"

"Mr. Dupree, what's this I hear about you trynna take some coochie?" Jonnea said.

"Damn, you ignorant," Keith said in the background.

"Shut up, white boy," Jonnea snapped at Keith. "Mr. Dupree, Keith asked me to start dreadlocks for him. I tried to tell that fool his hair too stringy. You've been gone for three days and this boy thinks he's Eminem."

"Jonnea," Dallas said, shaking his head. "What am I gonna do with you?"

"I'm just saying. Now, back to you. What's up with that little trick lying on you like that? Anybody with eyes could see how she used to be all over you. I'mma kick her ass if she comes back."

"Jonnea, I want you to go to the bathroom and wash your mouth out with soap."

"I'm sorry, Mr. Dupree. I'm just mad."

"Sorry, nothing. You cuss again and I'm coming up there and jack you up."

"For real? I'll cuss if that'll make you come back."

"Girl, you are too much."

"Stop saying that. I just wanted to let you know we love you and we don't believe that bullsh—"

"Jonnea!"

"Okay. Okay. Calm down. But you got to come on back. Don't be shamed. We all done been locked up one time or another. Oh, my momma told me to tell you she'll give you some. She said you ain't gotta go taking it."

"Tell your mother thanks, but no thanks. And tell her I haven't taken anything. Why aren't you guys in class?"

"Cuz we wanted to talk to you. We just bum-rushed the office and made the secretary call. You know she new, and she still scared."

Dallas smiled so wide that his face began to hurt. It felt good to have the support of his kids.

"Well, thank you, but now it's time for y'all to go back to class," he said. "And don't give the substitute a hard time. How you guys act is a direct reflection on me. Don't make me look bad."

"Yeah, yeah, yeah. We love you," Jonnea said.

"I love y'all too. Now, I gotta go. I'm getting another call."

"Bye, Mr. Dupree, " Jonnea said. Keith and D.J. yelled their good-byes in the background.

After saying farewell, Dallas clicked over to the other call.

"Mr. Dupree. How are you?" Yolanda Ross said.

"I'm fine. How are you?"

"I'm well, but I have a bit of bad news."

"I'm listening," he said.

"You said you couldn't remember if you'd had sex with Ms. Greer or not."

"That's right."

"Well, your semen was found on her sheets. Also, your blood tested positive for a controlled substance."

"What kind of controlled substance?" Dallas asked, confused.

"I'm not sure what it is right now, but the lab should get back to me by this afternoon."

"So, where do we go from here?"

"I'm heading over now to speak with the prosecution to see what evidence they have. I don't mean to sound pessimistic, but you might want to brace yourself for a trial."

Trial?

Dallas's heart sank all the way down to the floor. That one word hollowed him out. He couldn't trust a trial. He had seen too many times when the legal system failed people with his complexion, regardless of their innocence.

All of a sudden he wasn't feeling too well.

"Mr. Dupree . . ." Yolanda Ross said, snapping Dallas out of his thoughts.

"Yeah," he said, his voice just above a whisper.

"We'll be okay. Just have a little faith."

"This doesn't look good, does it?"

"I can't say. I have to speak with the prosecution first and see what evidence they have. Just think positively, and we'll get to the bottom of this."

Dallas ran his fingers through his hair and closed his eyes.

"Mr. Dupree, do you use drugs?"

"No," he snapped.

"Good," she said. "Were you using on the night in question?"

"No," he snapped again. "Didn't I just tell you I don't use drugs?"

"Mr. Dupree, I want you to listen to me," Yolanda said with a firmness Dallas hadn't heard before. "I'm on your side. Now, there will be times when I'm going to ask you questions that might make you a little uncomfortable, but please don't take it personally. I'm only trying to gather facts that will ultimately help you. Are we on the same page?"

Dallas sighed. "Yeah. Sorry for snapping on you. It's just . . . well this is some . . ." Dallas got up and walked out of the room so his niece and daughter couldn't hear his conversation. "This is crazy."

"I understand, but we'll get through it. Now, I have to run, but call me on my cell if you have anything else you want to discuss. I'm not coming back into the office once I leave this afternoon," Yolanda said.

Yeah, we don't wanna make you late for your dance class, Dallas thought.

Once again, he wondered if he was doing the right thing by keeping her on as his counsel. His life was in this woman's hands. He looked down at his white shirt and noticed it was covered with little black lines. He had been pulling his hair out. Stress had been a constant companion ever since he'd been arrested.

"Oh, Mr. Dupree, how is your niece?" Yolanda said.

"She's fine."

"Good. But one more thing. I'm going to need you to stay focused while this case is active, which means that when we set up an appointment I need you to keep it."

"No problem."

"Having gotten that out of the way, I want to say, I think it's pretty

noble of you to put your problems aside and take care of your family mat-
ters. It says a lot about you."

"Yeah, well, it is what it is," Dallas said, impatient to get off the phone
with this bossy little something.

"Okay. I'll call you soon."

Dallas hung up the phone with Yolanda and called Genesis.

"Hello," Genesis answered.

"Man, your sister dissed me," Dallas said, skipping the formalities.
"She gave my file to some low-budget lawyer in training."

"Whoa," Genesis said. "Hold up, brah. What are you talking about?"

"She assigned my file to this *girl*, and I mean *girl*. She sounds like a
baby and has only been a lawyer for two years. I have underwear older
than that."

"Damn, Dallas, you need to throw them things out."

"Man, I ain't in the mood for jokes."

"A'ight. I'll give Phyllis a call to see what's up."

"Thanks. I mean, I appreciate you looking out for me but I can't take
any chances with this thing."

"I feel you," Genesis said.

Dallas relaxed a bit. "How's the family?"

"Everybody is cool. I think Terri has moved back in. She hasn't said
anything but a lot of her clothes are in my closet and mine have somehow
been moved to the guest room," Genesis said. Dallas could hear the happiness in his friend's voice. "How is little Aja doing?"

"Aww, man, she's in hog heaven. My niece is over here and she's all but
forgotten about me."

"That's how they do. Whenever Terri is here Gabrielle acts like I'm
the enemy. That is until she wants something, then its 'Da-ddyyyyyy,
please!'"

Dallas laughed. He knew the feeling. "It's them little girls, man. They got us wrapped around their fingers and they know it. We gotta get us some little boys."

"Man, if I mention having a baby to Terri I'm liable to get slapped. I'm still on shaky ground."

"Oh yeah, you might wanna let her bring that subject up. I'm surprised you don't have about fifty kids, as much whoring as you did."

"Yeah, but those days are long gone. It's all about Terri now. Man, I can't remember the last time I was with another woman. Or any woman, 'cause Terri still on that wait-until-marriage thing. But she's worth it, so the dog can wait."

"That's good, brah. I'm proud of you. Give your sister a call and beg her to take over this case for me."

"I'll do it. You hang on in there, brah. Keep your head up."

"You know it. Give Terri and Gabrielle a hug for me," Dallas said.

Ten minutes later, Genesis's sister Phyllis called Dallas.

"Hello. May I speak to Mr. Dupree?" she said.

"This is he."

"Phyllis Pryor. How are you?"

"Not too good. I'm not too sure about the lawyer you delegated my case to."

"What's the problem?"

"I don't feel she has enough experience to handle my case. Plus I don't think she's devoting enough time to the case—she leaves at three in the afternoon."

"Mr. Dupree"—Phyllis spoke calmly—"we take a lot of pride in servicing our clients, and I can assure you that your case is being handled with the highest quality and professionalism. Ms. Ross is a very, very good attorney. She has one of the best legal minds I've come across, and is wise beyond her years. As a matter of fact, I pulled her from another case so that she could work on yours as a favor for my brother."

Dallas listened but didn't respond.

"I'll go so far as to say you are in the best hands this firm has to offer. She's a bit unorthodox but she gets the job done."

"What do you mean unorthodox?"

"She's a creative person who thinks outside the box. I just have to ask you to trust her. We most certainly do."

"Okay," Dallas said, still not fully convinced, but he figured if the head of the firm was giving her all that praise he would give her a shot.

"And if you are worried about her leaving the office at three in the afternoon, she comes in at four in the morning. That's an eleven-hour workday. You'll be fine, Mr. Dupree."

"Okay, but I want you to know that I'm innocent. Now, I know everyone says that, but I wouldn't do anything like what I'm accused of."

"Based on what my brother has said about you, I don't think you would either."

"Thanks a lot for calling and listening, Phyllis. I feel better already."

"I'm glad, Dallas. You try to enjoy your day," Phyllis said, and they hung up.

Dallas sat still for a moment, then he decided not to let his troubles bother him any more today. He laid down on the floor with his daughter and niece and grabbed a doll baby to try his hand at cosmetology.

TRUTH OR LIES

*P*riest paced the pastor's office as he waited for Kenya. He looked at his watch and realized he had been waiting for more than thirty minutes. He walked out of the office and down a small hallway and noticed no one was there. He walked to another office and saw a group of people on their knees praying.

These are the prayingest people I've ever seen, he thought.

Priest waited until they were finished, then he walked into the room. He recognized Kenya right away from her photo.

"May I have a minute of your time?" he asked. He'd formed his words as a question but anyone in earshot could tell that he expected cooperation.

"Do you know me?" Kenya asked.

Priest didn't answer. He just narrowed his eyes and

motioned with his head for her to stand up and follow him. Kenya didn't move.

Priest knew her kind, and he didn't plan on spending a lot of time playing games with her. He pulled back his jacket, showing the handle of his gun.

"What kind of man brings a gun into the house of the Lord?" Kenya said.

"Get up," he ordered.

Kenya looked around but it seemed that everyone had gotten busy all of a sudden.

Pastor Theofis was about to say something but Priest tilted his head, daring him to utter a single word.

Kenya looked at her pastor, then she grudgingly walked out the door.

"Follow me," Priest said.

"Who are you?"

"I'm a man with very little patience," Priest said, grabbing Kenya by her arms. "Now, let's set a few ground rules: I ask the questions, you give the answers. Are we straight?"

Kenya didn't respond.

"Nod your head."

Kenya nodded and her eyes betrayed her. She was scared.

They walked out of the small shotgun church.

"My name is Priest Dupree. You recognize the last name?"

Kenya stopped in her tracks. She turned to run but Priest held her arm.

"I'm not supposed to talk to anyone," she said.

"Oh, you gonna talk, or I'll send your ass to hell, cut up," Priest said, keeping his voice level. "Now, before you tell me what happened between you and my brother, I need to tell you a few things. Get in."

Priest opened the passenger door to his Mercedes. After he shut Kenya's door, he walked around to the driver's side and slid behind the wheel.

"My brother is a great man," Priest said, shifting in his seat so he faced Kenya. "I love him to death and there is nothing I wouldn't do for him."

Kenya remained silent.

"I know him better than anyone in this world and I know he wouldn't do what you said he did. Now, the question I have for you is, why?"

"Why, what?"

"Why are you lying?"

"I'm not," Kenya said, unable to meet his eyes.

Priest had seen many liars during his years on the force, and he knew from experience that there was one sitting in his passenger's seat.

"You weren't listening to me, were you?"

"You weren't there!" she shouted.

"Okay, you wanna do this the hard way, huh?" Priest started the car. He slowly pulled out of the parking lot.

"You must be some kind of fool if you think you're scaring me," Kenya challenged. "There is a church full of people who saw me leave with you."

Priest opened his hand and backhanded Kenya across her face. The force made her head hit the headrest. When she came forward her nose was bleeding and she immediately reached for the door. It was locked. She started banging on the window and Priest grabbed a handful of her hair and pulled her toward him.

"You better calm that ass down. You're not going anywhere," he said.

Kenya stared at him with a combination of fear and hatred on her face, but there weren't any tears.

"So, you gonna kidnap me and make me say your brother didn't rape me?"

"Nah, I'mma make you tell the truth."

"I told the truth. You just don't want to believe it. Your brother is an animal. You may not know him as well as you think you do."

"Oh, I know him. It's you that I'm wary of."

"Well, thank God that the world doesn't revolve around what you think."

"What is your relationship with Lord Jamal?"

Kenya's eyes almost popped out of their sockets. She looked straight ahead and started fidgeting.

"Is there something you wanna tell me?"

Suddenly the tears Priest had expected to see when he slapped her made their appearance.

"What's his relationship to this little lovely lady?" Priest tossed a picture of Kenya's eight-year-old daughter onto her lap.

All of a sudden her eyes pleaded for something.

"You wanna talk now?"

Kenya seemed to be in another world.

"I'll let you in on a little secret," Priest said as he turned the car into the parking lot of an abandoned building.

"Get out," he said as he exited the vehicle.

Kenya got out and stood beside the car.

"I know what happened. And you're going to prison for your little part in this."

"Prison?" Kenya started shaking her head from side to side. "I can't go to prison. I have kids."

"You should've thought about that when you agreed to be a part of this little charade," Priest said.

"Mister, I didn't have a choice. Jamal made me do it. He said he would put our daughter on the streets if I didn't do it," Kenya cried.

"And you think he would put his own child out on the streets?"

"If you knew so much, how come you don't know that he already has two of his daughters out there tricking? I didn't have a choice."

"What does my brother have to do with this?"

"It ain't about him. It's about you. He said you took all of his girls from him and ruined his life, so he wanted to ruin yours. He said you were the reason he had to put his own kids on the streets. Said something about you put the word out that he was a snitch and nobody wanted to work with him. So he asked me to get a job up at the school with Dallas," Kenya said, swallowing hard, "and to get him back to my place. At first he said he was going to kidnap him or kill him but he got arrested the same day we went out so he called and told me to do what I did." She was crying now. "I didn't have a choice. Please, mister. He was going to put my baby out on the streets."

"You know what?" Priest said, shaking his head. "This isn't adding up. I don't think my brother would agree to go back to your place. If he's going to be with you more than likely it would be at his place."

"He didn't agree."

"What do you mean?"

"I put some stuff Jamal gave me in his drink and he passed out."

"He passed out? How did his semen get on your sheets if he was asleep?"

Kenya looked down at the ground, embarrassed.

"I sucked him off while he was asleep."

Priest shook his head. "And y'all ignorant asses thought that would fly?"

Kenya didn't look up.

"Why didn't you just call the police about Jamal's threats?"

"I did. They told me they couldn't do anything on my word alone," she said.

"That's a lie, and you know it."

"I swear to you. I called the police twice. They don't pay me any attention anymore because I've called them so many times already about Jamal."

Priest thought about what he had heard and knew she was telling the truth. There were women who would call the police on their boyfriends about abuse, but would usually end up taking them back. After a while, the police would stop taking the calls seriously.

"Okay, I'll tell you what you're going to do."

Kenya shook her head to thwart off any plans Priest was making. "He's going to hurt my baby!"

"Nah, I'm going to make sure Jamal never hurts another soul," Priest said, walking back around to the driver's side. "Get in."

There was something about Kenya that reminded him of Mina when they first met. He believed her and even though he was furious with her for getting Dallas caught up in this mess, he sympathized with her.

"Does he have custody of your daughter?"

"No, she lives with his sister. I wasn't able to keep her when I had her, but I got myself together now and I'm trying to get her back."

"We're going to take a trip downtown and you're going to tell the prosecutor what you just told me. You're going to ask him for a dismissal form so you can straighten this mess out with my brother. As far as Jamal goes, you don't have anything to worry about." Priest couldn't wait to pay a visit to his old nemesis.

NO LOVE

*C*armen sat on the chaise in her bedroom. She was wearing the same nightgown she'd worn for the past two days. She rarely moved and only got up to shower and use the bathroom. She stared out the window at the rain dancing under the streetlights and willed herself not to cry. She had no more tears left.

Being alone was so hard. Everyplace she turned there were memories of Sterling. His shirts, his pants, his boots, a book he was reading, and his scent. His scent was the one thing that drove her the craziest. The day he left with Priest, she'd washed just about everything that could be washed, yet his scent still remained.

Carmen ran her hand across her stomach and wondered where the father of her child could be. Was he alive? Did those men find him? Was he thinking about her? The least he could've done was call. Carmen stood up and moved to the love seat, where she and Sterling would often snuggle. But now those times were long gone. And she wasn't even sure how much of those times were genuine. But the one thing she did know was that she had been a fool. How could she allow herself to believe that someone as good-looking as Sterling could fall for someone like her? Every time she thought about how she'd been used the floodgates threatened to open up again.

Not much in her personal life had changed since the days when she would allow the boys in the projects to touch her breasts just so she could feel the energy of being wanted.

From as far back as Carmen could remember she'd struggled with her weight. At a size eighteen, she wasn't society's ideal. She had tried almost every diet that ever hit the market, but ultimately found that she couldn't alter genetics.

Just when she thought she was destined to live a life of loneliness, Sterling came along. And with the exception of her brothers, he was the first man to make her feel good about herself. He courted her as if she were a princess and it felt good. It felt damn good to finally be wanted, and, to top it off, by a man so sexy other women openly gawked. So after a few weeks of roses, dinners, movies, and just plain old chivalry, she was his for the taking. But she always expected that one day he'd call and say that he'd made a mistake, that he'd found someone else, but it never happened. Then he did what she thought no man would ever do—he asked her to marry him. It was real. She was so excited. Yes, it was real, and for the first time in her life she allowed herself to believe in a man other than her brothers. Someone did want her. But now she realized that it had all been a lie.

Carmen stood and trudged down the stairs. It took all the strength she had. A broken heart was a hard thing to carry. But she knew she had to think about the baby, and she needed to eat.

The phone rang on her way to the kitchen. She saw it was Dallas and she let the call go to her voice mail. Two minutes later it rang again; this time it was Priest and he got the voice mail treatment too.

Carmen removed a few pieces of tilapia and seasoned them to perfection. Carmen forced herself to think about happy things. Anything that would ease her broken heart. Then, like the angel she was, Carmen's mother's voice flooded Carmen's head.

Baby, never love a man more than you love yourself. Unless you bore that baby who became a man.

The voice was so clear Carmen looked around to see if her mother was in the house. All of a sudden she felt better. Her mother was right. It was time to start reclaiming her feelings. Besides, Sterling had already taken enough from her. She dropped a few teaspoons of water into a frying pan, added half a bag of spinach leaves and some Goya seasoning, and covered the pan. The oven beeped to let her know it was preheated. And just as she put the fish in, the doorbell rang. She ignored it. It was probably one of her neighbors coming over to check on her, but she didn't want to see anyone. Then she heard a voice calling out to her from the backyard. The voice frightened her. It was him. It was Sterling. Carmen froze. He called out again and tapped on the kitchen window. Startled, Carmen jumped back and placed a hand over her chest.

What should she do? What could she do?

Carmen walked over to the back door and flung it open. There he was. Sterling was standing on her porch looking like hell. His clothes were rumpled, and his hair was uncombed. His eyes were still dark with bruises. Carmen stared at him and he stared back with pitiful eyes.

"Why?" was all she could muster through her tears.

"Can I come in?" he said, looking over his shoulder.

"Why, Sterling?"

"Carmen, I'm sorry, baby. Things got out of hand but I never meant to hurt you," he said, easing closer to the door. "I love you."

Carmen stared at the man who, just a few days ago, was the center of her life. She couldn't explain what she felt at that moment.

Before he'd shown up, all she wanted was for him to come back. It didn't matter what Priest would think. He was her brother, not her father. It was her life and she wanted her husband home. Who could blame her for wanting to raise her child with two parents under one roof? Who could tell her that it was okay to be alone, to go back to not being wanted? No one! On the other hand, she would rather raise her child alone than put him or her in harm's way by allowing a trifling man to linger around. After all, he had allowed their home to be violated by his thuggish associates. Yes indeed, there was a very thin line between love and hate.

Carmen's legs took on a mind of their own and she stepped back to allow Sterling to enter.

"Thank you, baby." Sterling smiled and hustled his way past Carmen. "Something smells good," he said as he ran straight up the stairs. Carmen stood still holding the door open until she heard the water from the shower upstairs. She had wanted to stop him, had opened her mouth and held up a hand to halt his movements, but nothing had come out.

She closed the door and locked it. Her husband was home. Good, bad, or indifferent. He was hers and she wanted him there.

Carmen sat at the table and tried to get ahold of her emotions. She felt like a hopeless prisoner in her own home. There was a man upstairs in her bedroom who was still her husband, but something deep inside of her said he wasn't supposed to be there. Sterling walked down the stairs wearing only a pair of underwear. He came into the kitchen, leaned on the counter, and folded his arms.

"I see you didn't throw my things out," he said with a smile. "What are you cooking?"

Carmen stared at Sterling as if he'd lost his mind.

"Is that all you have to say?" she said, still looking at him strangely.

"Come on, Carmen, I said I was sorry. People make mistakes. Haven't you ever made a mistake?"

Yes, marrying you. She pushed that thought aside. "So, how long have you had this problem?"

"I don't have a problem. I said it was a mistake," Sterling snapped, walking out of the kitchen and back into the living room. "I'm hungry."

Carmen followed him out to the living room.

"Don't you think we need to talk?"

"We already did."

"No," Carmen said, shaking her head. "We need to have a heart-to-heart."

"Carmen, I'm hungry. Do you think we can talk over dinner?"

Carmen sighed and decided that maybe that could work. She turned and headed back toward the kitchen, but as she passed a mirror hanging on the wall she saw Sterling sticking his middle finger up at her. *That immature bastard.* Was that all he thought about her? After all the pain he'd caused, he still could find enough selfishness in him to suggest that she go and screw herself? He was playing her, and Carmen had had enough. She turned around and started toward Sterling. He must've seen the look in her eyes, because he jumped up.

"Get out!" she said, pointing toward the door.

"I ain't going nowhere!"

"Leave!" she screamed.

"Take your ass in that kitchen and fix me something to eat," he snapped.

Finally, the real Sterling!

Carmen stopped. She was frozen in place. Was he talking to her?

"Don't look at me crazy," Sterling barked. "Now, I said I'm hungry, and I'm not going to ask you again."

Yeah, he was talking to her.

"What you gonna do, run and call your brother? I can handle that nigga too."

All of the hurt and rage came to a head and she snapped. She picked up the lamp and threw it at Sterling. He ducked and leaped across the coffee table and was on her before she could move. He grabbed her neck and backed her up until she hit the wall. He used his free hand to slap her hard across the face. Carmen closed her eyes and his grip tightened around her neck. She started to gasp.

"Now, what did I ask you to do for me?"

Carmen felt around for a weapon, any weapon. Her hand found a marble bookend on the edge of her desk. She lifted it high and brought it down as hard as she could on the side of Sterling's head. His grip went limp and he fell to the floor. Carmen leaned over, trying to catch her breath. She stepped over Sterling's body, made it to the phone and dialed 911.

"I need the police."

28

FREE

*D*allas drove Kameka back to the same high school she had attended before Laquita sent her to live with Carmen. He waited patiently while she reregistered herself. He was impressed with her maturity and how well she handled herself. Students and faculty alike gravitated toward her as if she was the prodigal daughter.

"Are you some kind of superstar around here?" Dallas asked, taking in the scene.

"Nah, these are my people," Kameka said, hugging folks as they came along. "I'm going to miss this place."

"One more year and you're all done, huh? It's time to start choosing a college," Dallas said.

Kameka nodded. "But this is my last year, Uncle Dallas. I'm a senior."

"Since when? You're only sixteen," Dallas asked, confused.

"I went to summer school every year just to get out of my mom's house, so now I'm only three classes shy of graduating."

"Kameka, you're messing with me, right?"

She shook her head.

"Why didn't you tell somebody?"

Kameka shrugged it off. "Didn't have anyone to tell. You know my mom could care less, and y'all . . . ," she started with a knowing smile. "Well, you know."

Yes, he knew. As an uncle he sucked, and Priest sucked and Carmen sucked. They didn't step up and do the right thing by their niece. Sure, they would send her gifts on birthdays and Christmas and maybe drop her a few guilty dollars in the mail, but that's not what she needed. She needed them. As an educator he knew firsthand how kids spelled love: T.I.M.E.

Kameka smiled.

"It's all good, though. We're straight now," she said, balling up her fist and lightly tapping knuckles with her uncle. They were cool like that. "Now I better get my butt to class."

"When I pick you up today, I'm going to bring you a little surprise."

Kameka smiled from ear to ear. "I like surprises."

"What time do you get out of here, since you only have three classes?"

"Oh, I'm here all day. I'm a math tutor for a few of the freshmen and sophomores."

"So what's up with college?"

"I'm going to an out of state school. Preferably Duke. That is if my mom will ever fill out the daggone paperwork for my financial aid."

Dallas was beside himself. He was so proud of his niece and realized he and his siblings were really the ones who missed out. She was so much more than what she allowed the outside world to see. They missed out on watching a very special little girl grow into a beautiful and intelligent young lady.

"I'll catch the MARTA bus over to your house after school," Kameka said.

"*Home*," Dallas said, giving her a hug. "You'll catch the MARTA bus *home.*"

Kameka nodded and smiled. "I'll catch the MARTA bus home. Go on, Uncle Dallas. You act like I'm going off to war or something," she said before walking off down the hall.

Dallas ignored his niece's instructions and stood there until she disappeared around a corner. She was something else, and she wouldn't be needing any financial aid. He would make sure of that. Plus he was going to surprise her with that Lexus convertible that Yasmin would never make it home to drive.

WHEN DALLAS got back to his truck he checked the messages on his cell phone. There were three messages from his lawyer, asking him to come and meet her at some dance studio. She left the address and Dallas punched it into his vehicle's navigational system.

Ten minutes later he was parked in front of a building with a hand-painted sign that read THE YOLANDA ROSS DANCE COMPANY.

What the . . . ? he thought. *I'm not feeling this Savion Glover/lawyer crap.*

Dallas walked into the cozy little spot and the receptionist pointed him toward a glass door. He opened the door and stepped into a wide-open room with shiny hardwood floors. Rails and mirrors were on every wall except the back wall, which was covered with a mural of a lady with about fifty kids, all standing on their little tippy toes.

Dallas knew right away the lone dancer in the room was Yolanda Ross. He leaned against a wall and watched her. He wasn't a big fan of ballet but she was good. Her movements were fluid. She was poetry in motion. She smiled at him and kept on with her routine until the music stopped. She did a little curtsy to complete her routine, then she slowly walked over and extended a hand.

"Mr. Dupree. Yolanda Ross. Nice to meet you. Finally."

"Likewise," Dallas said, shaking her hand. She didn't look at all like he thought she'd look. He pictured some nerdy little lady wearing thick glasses. How wrong he was. This woman was beautiful, and the white tights she wore showed that she had curves in all the right places. Her face was a smooth mahogany brown. And she had a bald head. Not closely cropped but bald. Bald, like Michael Jordan, but it fit her perfectly. She had large, full lips and high cheekbones. She was striking—and she reminded him of Yasmin.

"What's up?" he asked, snapping out of his visual fantasy. After all, this wasn't a social visit.

She smiled. "I have some good news and a bit of bad news."

Here we go, Dallas thought.

"The good news is the young lady who brought these charges against you has suddenly had a change of heart. Somehow she now remembers your evening together altogether differently."

Dallas couldn't believe his ears. Was he hearing her correctly? He couldn't stop smiling. He was almost afraid to ask her the bad news.

"The bad news is the prosecutor is a butt hole and wants the state to take over the case. He thinks she was coerced into changing her statement."

"Huh?" Dallas asked. The fear that he'd been walking around with came rushing back. "Why would he think that?"

Yolanda held up both palms and tilted her head. "Don't know, but that's his issue."

"So what do we do now?"

"You live your life. I'll take care of the prosecutor. He knows this is just a tactic to save face. I'll destroy him if he tries to move on this." Yolanda Ross smiled. "Congratulations, and I'm really sorry that you had to go through this."

"Congratulations? But you just said they were still going to prosecute me."

"Mr. Dupree, what did I just tell you? Have a little faith in me. They'll call me and officially drop the case, or you'll own this city."

"So you're saying this is over?"

"Pretty much."

Dallas wanted to leap up and kiss the sky. He reached out and hugged Yolanda. She gave him a nice little embrace in return.

"Do you want to have dinner with me tonight?"

"I can't do that."

"Why?"

"Well, for one, you are a client, and I don't mix business with pleasure. Two, I have to prepare a routine for my kids. We're going to New York to a dance competition and I'm way behind the power curve."

"I see. Well, I appreciate what you've done and I must say I underestimated you," Dallas said, looking around the studio. "I even called your boss."

"And called me incompetent." Yolanda smiled again. "I heard all about it."

"Hey, she wasn't supposed to tell you that."

Yolanda held her smile and shook her head as if to say she'd heard it all before.

"Being a lawyer is what I do. Being a dancer is who I am. I love them both."

"Do your thing, girl," Dallas said, nodding his head. "If you don't mind, would you keep my cell phone number? That way, once I'm officially not a client anymore, I can take you to lunch, if that's okay with you."

Yolanda didn't respond. She just reached out and shook his hand. She walked to the back of the room where the stereo was mounted and turned it on. Hip-hop music mixed with classical came on and she went into a routine that would surely give Debbie Allen a run for her money. Dallas watched her and the more he saw her move the more he wanted to see of her, but he tried to push the thoughts from his mind.

I'm tripping. Why would she want to go out with a guy who was just accused of raping somebody, Dallas thought before turning to walk out.

"Oh, and Mr. Dupree," Yolanda said over the music. "I found out what was in your bloodstream. It was a drug called Myronoxidol. It renders you unconscious and unless you are a miracle man, you didn't have sex with Ms. Greer. At least not that night."

"What about the semen?"

Yolanda smiled again. "Gotta give the girl some credit. She has skills. You have a good day, Mr. Dupree."

Dallas shook his head and walked out of the building. There were still so many unanswered questions, but he was just happy this thing was over.

"This just in. The Alonzo Crim High School teacher who was accused of sexual assault was exonerated today. Y'all know that fine specimen of a man—Mr. Dallas Dupree. The charges were false. In other words, the chick flat-out lied," Porche Foxx, the afternoon radio personality on V-103, was saying on the radio when Dallas turned out of the dance company parking lot. "Go Dallas, it's your birthday. Go Dallas, it's your birthday. Now, come on up here and holla at a sister."

Dallas couldn't help but smile. It wasn't his birthday, but he closed his eyes and wished for Kenya Greer to find some peace. He wanted to hate her for everything she'd put him through, but it just wasn't in him.

Dallas turned the radio off and drove toward Alonzo Crim High School in total silence. At every red light he bowed his head and thanked God for getting him out of this mess. He turned into the school's parking lot and was greeted by a huge sign hanging over the front door that read WE LOVE YOU, MR. DUPREE!

He smiled as he stared at the sign. "And I love ya back."

29

Priest and Baldhead rode around the Bluff in a beat-up hooptie. They were looking for one man and one man only—Lord Jamal.

"Priest, I hear this boy is off the chain. You need to give me a gun," Baldhead said.

"Not a chance, Mario. You know how you like to go overboard. Plus, I don't know where you're getting your information from these days but he's not off the chain. He's a little punk."

"Overboard? I know you ain't talking. What did Dallas say when you told him what went down with that Kenya chick?"

"He didn't say anything, but you know Dallas. He wants this world to be heaven, so I gotta raise hell to give it to him."

"Yeah, Dallas is one of those rare dudes. Except

sometimes he gets to messing up. Like when he got the mayor to sign off on that crap about not opening the liquor stores until five o'clock," Baldhead said, shaking his head. "What kind of foolishness is that?"

Priest laughed. "I liked that one."

"Yeah, cuz you don't drink. Shit, I gotta wait around all damn day just to get my drink on. I might as well go get a job."

"Exactly," Priest said, shaking his head.

They rode down a few more streets in silence, both lost in their own thoughts.

"So, this Lord Jamal cat really had it in for you, huh?"

"I guess so. Some brothers are obsessed with being trifling. Now, here is a dude who grew up with two educated parents but still turned out to be a pimp. How did that happen? Then when I tried to force him to do the right thing, he flipped out."

"So, now he's obsessed with getting you back for making him stop pimping."

"Oh, he's a stone fool. Got his own kids out there screwing dudes to put some money in his sorry-ass pockets. Yeah, he's gonna get his today. Then I'm locking him up."

"Now, Priest, don't you go overboard," Baldhead cautioned sarcastically.

Priest smiled at his friend. "Me?"

"Speaking of overboard, how you just gonna leave me in jail?"

Priest laughed again.

"Oh, you think it's funny, huh?"

"That's right. Who told you to get yourself locked up?"

"I was looking out for Dallas. You know he would've been in there trying to philosophize with those dumb niggas."

"Dallas can handle himself."

"That ain't the point. He ain't cut out for that jail crap. Remind me to slap the taste outta your mouth when this is over," Baldhead said. "Okay?"

"I'll do that," Priest said, shaking his head. It was good to hang with his old friend again.

"You know what they say about guys spending too much time in jail, don't you?" Baldhead said, touching Priest's right thigh. He batted his eyes and took a bite at him.

"Mario, you got two seconds to get your dick beaters off of me," Priest said, trying not to laugh.

"Come on, big daddy, I missed hanging out with you. Just rolling around with ya gets me all moist inside."

"Get your damn hands off of me," Priest said, swinging at Baldhead's hand. "See, that's why you're not getting a gun. You play too much."

Baldhead snatched his hand back and cracked up laughing.

"Priest, you need an anger management class."

Priest turned into the driveway of a house next door to the one his snitch had pointed out as the residence of Lord Jamal.

"This is it, brah," Priest said, all business now. "Let's do this."

As soon as the car stopped, Baldhead hit the ground running. He walked up to the front door and knocked. Priest hurried around to the side.

"Who is it?" a male voice said.

"Lord, this George Bush. Let me holla at you," Baldhead said, giving the street name of another pimp. "I got some split tails I need to holla at you about."

The door opened and Lord Jamal stood there dressed only in a pair of satin boxers. He had gold teeth and his hair was in pink rollers.

"Check this out, baby," Baldhead said, removing a gun from his waistband and pointing it at Jamal. "Bring that ass on out here."

Priest saw what was going on and cursed. He wanted to kill Baldhead.

This was not the proper way to bring a suspect down. Jamal dropped to the floor and tried to close the door. Baldhead stuck his foot in between the door and the frame to keep the door open. He grimaced in pain as the door slammed against his foot.

Priest jumped up on the porch and tried to force the door back open. Jamal released the door and ran to a back room and slammed the door shut. Priest gave Baldhead a look before entering the house. They didn't know if anyone else was in the house, so they proceeded with caution.

Once they were both in the house, they positioned themselves on either side of the bedroom door. "Why you gotta do things your way?" Priest snapped.

Before Baldhead could respond there was a loud explosion and shards of wood from the door went flying everywhere.

"Get down," Priest barked.

"That's why," Baldhead said, ducking down from a second blast. "You trynna send me to a gunfight without a damn gun."

"That's a double-barrel. Go back outside and take the back," Priest said, getting down low as he crawled into the bedroom.

Jamal had one leg outside of the window when Priest shouted, "Don't move." He had his gun pointed at Jamal.

Jamal looked at Priest with a surprised expression. Then that look turned to pure hatred and Jamal swept his arm around and unloaded an arsenal in Priest's direction. It sounded like the Fourth of July in the little house.

Priest covered his head and then felt the hot sensation as one of the bullets penetrated his calf. Another one hit him in the upper part of the back of his thigh. He felt another bullet but he couldn't tell where he was hit. Priest rolled back out of the room and prayed Jamal didn't come after him. The pain was unbearable. He wanted to yell but he couldn't. He lay still, trying to focus on something pleasant. He thought about his brother and his sister and how well both of them were doing. Then he had a visual of his mother and his brother Antoine waving him into a clouded room. Priest ran his hand over his stomach and felt a thick liquid. Blood was everywhere. He felt dizzy. He was getting weak. Then there was blackness.

Baldhead saw Jamal jump out the window with his gun still smoking. Jamal hit the ground and took off running. Baldhead expected to see Priest jump out the window after him to give chase, but he never appeared. That caused him to worry. Especially with all the shots fired. Now he wasn't sure if he should go after Jamal or go into the house to check up on Priest. He decided he would stop Lord Jamal and took off after him.

Jamal was running as if his life depended on it but he was no match for Baldhead, who was once a track star. Jamal turned around to fire his gun and lost his balance. He tumbled over and when he finally came to a stop Baldhead met him with a kick to the face. Baldhead kneeled down over Jamal and punched him in the face until the little man was a limp rag doll.

Baldhead removed the gun from Jamal's hand and stuck it into his waistband. He reached down and lifted the five foot three and barely a hundred pound Jamal like a grocery bag. He tossed him over his shoulder and headed back to the house. People were outside looking, but he didn't care. This was the Bluff, an impoverished section of Atlanta, and if there was anyplace where the police couldn't get a straight answer out of a resident, this was it.

Baldhead tossed Jamal in the trunk of the car like a pound of dirt from Home Depot.

Baldhead hurried into the house and saw his best friend lying in a pool of blood. He wasn't moving. Baldhead couldn't move either.

"Aww, nah," Baldhead managed, as he found his legs and walked over to check Priest's pulse.

Priest's hand was trembling, and he slowly opened his eyes.

"Did you get him?"

"Yeah, I got him. Don't talk, man. You need an ambulance," Baldhead said, reaching for the phone. It was disconnected.

Priest shook his head.

"What you want me to do?"

"Get me outta here," Priest said as he tried to sit up. Too much pain. He lay back down. Baldhead lifted him as best he could. Priest was a big man, and it took all the strength he could muster to drag him out of the house. He opened the passenger door and put the bucket seat in the horizontal position before laying Priest down.

"Call my sister," Priest said, his voice just above a whisper.

Baldhead punched in the digits on the cell phone. "Carmen, this is Mario. Priest was just shot."

"Shot?" Carmen yelled. "What . . . where are you? Where was he shot?" she asked, fear all in her voice.

"I can't tell. Blood is everywhere."

"Where are you?"

"We in the Bluff."

"Okay, get him to Grady. I'll have someone meet you in the emergency room. Stay on the phone with me."

Carmen barked instructions to Baldhead while he drove like a bat out of hell toward Grady Memorial Hospital. Priest wasn't talking, nor was he moving. He looked like he was sleeping.

"He ain't moving, Carm. What do I do?" Baldhead panicked.

"Just hurry up."

Baldhead pulled into the employee parking lot and ran straight through the wooden arm on the lot. He was met by two guys with a stretcher. They hurried over to the car and took Priest.

"He's gone," one of paramedics said, touching Priest's neck.

"Nooooo," Baldhead screamed.

"Sir, please stand back. He's lost his pulse," the guy said as they rushed Priest into the building through a set of sliding glass doors. Baldhead tried to follow but a security guard stopped him.

Baldhead waited until Carmen arrived. He gave her an update and she disappeared through the same doors that he wasn't allowed to enter. He had never cried a tear as a grown man, yet he couldn't stop them now. Priest was his brother, always had been and always would be. He had never met a more stand-up guy. Then he remembered that the man responsible for this tragedy was in the trunk of the car.

Baldhead walked out to the car. He opened the trunk and looked at the sorry excuse for a man.

"Jail is too good for your little narrow ass. Death is too, but you'll get it. Right now you need to suffer," Baldhead said to the still-unconscious Jamal. He looked around to make sure no one saw him. Then he flipped Jamal's limp body around and tied his hands behind his back with some duct tape. He opened up his toolbox and removed a pair of vice-grip pliers. He snatched the miniature man around and clamped down on his testicles and locked the pliers in place.

Jamal regained consciousness and screamed like a little girl but Baldhead slammed the trunk, muffling his cries. He walked around to the driver's side and got in. He looked over at the passenger seat, saw all of the blood, and closed his eyes in prayer for his friend. He grabbed Priest's cell phone and scrolled though the menu until he came to the name Sassy. Sassy stood a full seven feet two inches tall. He weighed three hundred and fifty pounds and he was proud to be a homosexual. Baldhead hit the send button.

"Sassy, this Mario."

"Talk to me," the man said, in a deep yet feminine voice.

"I'm on my way over there."

"Let me talk to Priest."

"He . . ." Baldhead struggled. "He's dead, man."

"Please tell me you didn't say what I thought you said," Sassy said.

"The cat I'm bringing over there shot him," Baldhead said, barely holding it together. "He shot him, man."

"Bring his ass to me," Sassy barked. "You get him over here. You get him here now."

Baldhead pulled up to Sassy's small house on the backstreet of a dilapidated neighborhood. Sassy walked out with tears in his eyes. He was a huge man with long blond hair that was pulled into a ponytail.

"Mario, you all right?"

Baldhead nodded. He couldn't believe his best friend was dead. This couldn't be.

"Where is he?"

Baldhead popped the trunk.

Jamal was conscious now and had somehow worked the pliers free from his private parts.

"What y'all niggas want with me?" Jamal said.

"Priest was my friend!" Sassy said, his hulking figure leaning toward Jamal.

Sassy thought back to his high school days when Priest was the only friend he had. Once he decided not to hide his sexuality, all of his so-called friends deserted him. Everyone except Priest. Priest never judged Sassy. Even when he found out he was HIV positive. He remained his friend.

"Fuck Priest," Lord Jamal said.

"No, sweetie," Sassy said, reaching out to offer Jamal a hand out of the trunk. "That's exactly what I plan to do to you. Now, come to daddy."

Jamal scooted as far back into the trunk as possible.

"Don't make me chase you," Sassy said calmly. "Embrace your fate. Life as you know it is over."

"Wait, man. Let me talk to you," Jamal screamed.

But Sassy never was a big talker. He slammed a huge paw down around Jamal's neck and dragged him from the trunk.

EPILOGUE

THREE MONTHS LATER

*T*hings have pretty much returned to normal for me. My students are still a little crazy, but I wouldn't have them any other way. Three weeks ago, I got a call from Ms. Yolanda Ross inviting me to one of her dance recitals. Afterward we enjoyed a romantic dinner at a cozy restaurant overlooking the Chattahoochee River. Have you ever met someone, and you just knew he or she was the right one for you? Well if not, y'all keep on searching; it'll happen. There's nothing like it in the world. And the funny thing is, I think Yasmin had a hand in sending Yolanda to me. Sounds crazy, but that's just how I feel. Today will be our twentieth date in just about as many days. What can I say, I like her li'l baldheaded self and even more important, Aja likes her. I was a little hesitant to let my little girl meet her this quickly, but I'm feeling her, and like I said before, it just feels right.

Today I'm taking Yolanda and Aja to Priest's house. Yep, three gunshot wounds and less one kidney, but he survived. Ya know I've learned to leave his business alone. If he wants to be a drug dealer and justify it by saying he only sells to the rich, then so be it. He's my brother, and I'm just happy to have him here.

As we pulled up the long winding driveway, I saw that Carmen and Kameka were already here. Kameka even parked her little Lexus perfectly. I don't know why but I feel proud every time I see her driving that car. Maybe it's guilt, I don't know—but whatever it is it's good for my soul. It took me long enough to teach her to pick a lane and stay in it, but now she drives like a pro. We just found out she was eligible for this HOPE scholarship, so Priest and I won't be out of too much money sending her wherever she decides to go to college. We refused to let Carmen participate in the funding of Kameka's education—after all, we have a new baby on the way. Plus, I think that's the man's thing to do.

"Man, hurry up," Priest said impatiently, sitting in his wheelchair in his doorway. "And give me my baby."

He reached out for Aja and she happily went to him.

"Your daddy is going to be late to his own funeral, you know that?"

"No." Aja giggled and nestled into her uncle.

"Oh, yes he is."

"What's up, dude?" I said, rubbing him on his head. He hates that and looked at me like I was crazy. So I did it again.

"Hey, Yolanda," he said, frowning but trying to be nice in front of his guest.

"Hey, Priest," Yolanda said. "How are you feeling?"

"Good enough to slap this boy if he touches my head one more time."

"Now, y'all be good," Mina said, walking down the hall. "Hey, everybody."

"Why you late?" Priest barked at me.

I looked at Yolanda and tried to toss the blame her way.

"Oh, no," she said, shaking her head. "You're not putting that on me. As I recall, Aja and I had to wait for you in the car."

"What's up, people?" Baldhead boomed as he walked in the door. He kissed Yolanda and Mina on the cheek and picked up Aja. "How's my folks?"

"Man, you late too, but you don't matter since you already know," Priest said, wheeling himself down the hallway into the den.

I couldn't take my eyes off of Baldhead. He was clean shaven and his hair was freshly cut. He wore what looked like a thousand-dollar suit and shoes to match.

"What the hell you looking at, Dallas?" he snapped. "You didn't know a brother could get snazzy?"

"Baldhead, I didn't even know you owned a suit," I said, still amazed at the major transformation.

"That ain't all you don't know," he said with a smirk on his face as we walked down the hall behind Priest.

"Mario," Priest warned. "Can you keep your mouth shut for ten more minutes?"

I sensed something was up and whatever it was, Baldhead almost ruined it.

"Mario, why do they call you Baldhead? You have more hair than me," Yolanda asked.

"Yolanda, I have news for you: Most people have more hair than you. Now don't get me wrong, cuz I swear you finer than frog hair," he said, causing everyone to laugh. "But nobody calls me that except this clown." Baldhead pointed at me. "He has mental issues. You better get him to a shrink before y'all go any further with whatever y'all doing."

We all walked into the den. Baldhead plopped down between Kameka and Carmen even though they were sitting close to each other.

"Hi, Mario." Carmen smiled, moving over to give him a little more room. "Don't you look nice."

"Baby, all this can be yours if you act right," he said. "I'm glad you got rid of that clown. You have no idea how it hurt my heart to see you with that buster."

"And you have no idea how much it hurt me when I found out you were using drugs," Carmen snapped.

"Now, see, why you gotta go there?" Baldhead looked around before leaning over and whispering something in Carmen's ear. A look of confusion crossed her face. Then she smiled.

"Hey, Meek," Baldhead said.

"Hey, Mario, how are you doing?" Kameka said as Aja crawled from Baldhead's lap into Kameka's arms. She was family.

"Girl, if I was any better I'd be sitting on God's lap," he said, throwing a leg over Carmen's leg. She didn't move it.

Priest yelled, "Okay, okay. Shut up. I got an announcement to make. Now, I know I haven't been the best brother or uncle lately but in a few minutes you'll understand why." He looked over his shoulder at the television. "There's a lot you guys don't know and hopefully I can clear everything up today. For one, today is my and Mina's one-year anniversary." Priest paused to let his words sink in.

Mina held up a sparkling diamond ring and everyone congratulated her with hugs and kisses.

"Only two people know what's really been going on with . . . " He stopped talking. He turned up the volume on his sixty-inch television as the afternoon news anchor came on.

"Today an Atlanta police officer has single-handedly pulled off the largest drug bust in Georgia's history. Pablo Escada was arrested today and five million dollars in cash and another million dollars' worth of drugs were confiscated. Officer Priest Dupree has spent the last three years working his way into the inner fibers of one of this country's most notorious drug cartels and today we see the fruits of his labor," Monica Kaughman said before the camera panned to Priest, who was seated at a podium.

"I won't take up much of your time and I don't mean to turn this into an awards ceremony but I really need to thank my family for hanging in there with me even when they didn't know who I was anymore. I do what I do because drugs have plagued our community for too long. I couldn't have done this without the help of my good friend Mario Jackson who worked the streets for two years pretending to be an addict for the cause. And I have to thank my sister, Dr. Carmen LaCour, for saving my life and being the best sister a guy could ask for. To my wife and my nieces, you'll see a new man. I promise. And last but not least, I have to thank my brother Dallas Dupree for simply being you. You are the best man I know," he said and gave the thumbs-up to the camera.

Priest turned around and faced me.

"What you think about that, Dallas?" he said, smiling.

I was speechless. I wanted to cry, but damn all that. Not in front of Baldhead. I'd never live it down. I was shocked but I should've known something wasn't right with Priest. I walked over and stood in front of my brother, smiling from ear to ear. He reached out to shake my hand. I wanted to pull him out of that chair and hug him until he suffocated, but instead I just rubbed his head. He grabbed my hand and tried to twist it. But just like the old days, Carmen made him stop.

"Okay, okay," Mina said, trying to get everyone's attention. "Kameka has an announcement to make."

Kameka got up, still holding Aja, and stood beside Mina.

"Sometimes I can't help but think about what I've missed by not being around my family." Kameka started crying. Carmen got up to comfort her, but Kameka held up her hand as if to ask for a moment to compose herself. "But, I don't want to dwell on the past. It feels so good to be here amongst family. So, I decided not to go to college out of state. I'm going to stay right here in Georgia and go to Spelman and let you all spoil me some more." Kameka smiled through her tears as Mina, Yolanda, and Carmen gathered around to hug her. Even Aja got in on the crying. I guess it's a woman thing. Kameka hugged everyone before sitting back down.

"Hey," Baldhead said, standing up. "Damn it, I got an announcement to make too. I am not a crackhead. Never was, never will be."

"Well, thank God for that," Carmen said, laughing through her tears and clapping her hands.

"Okay, everyone," Mina said. "Let's continue this celebration in the dining room. Kameka and I spent hours preparing this food, so eat up."

And that's just what we did. We talked about the good old days. Baldhead made everyone laugh with his crackhead stories. Then I felt like I needed a little quiet time so I walked out and stood on the deck. I was watching the ducks in the lake when Yolanda came out.

"I know he's going to miss this place," I said. "Hell, I'm going to miss this place."

"Why do you say that? Is he moving?"

"Well, I'm sure they are not going to let him keep all of this. Not on a detective's salary."

"Maybe, maybe not. The government has been after that guy for years. He'll be in line to receive a reward, which I know is over a million dollars. Priest may be able to stay here for as long as he wants."

"I guess you're right," I said, nodding.

"So everything isn't always what it seems after all, huh?"

I just shook my head. After the events of these past few months, I knew anything was possible.

"Are Mario and Carmen a couple?"

"Nah, but he's always had a thing for her. She likes him too. Now that we know he's not on drugs, maybe they'll hook up. Lord knows she deserves somebody good, and Baldhead is just like family, so that would be just perfect."

"They look sweet together," she said.

"Somehow I wouldn't put Baldhead and sweet in the same sentence," I said.

"Stop it. He's a very kind man."

"Yeah, Baldhead is good people. He should be an actor because he pulled that crackhead thing off better than Samuel L. Jackson in *Jungle Fever*."

Yolanda looked inside the house at Baldhead, who looked to be surgically attached to Carmen's right side.

"They are too cute together."

"Carmen is going through a divorce right now, so I'm sure Baldhead will be helping her through her trying times," I said.

"So," she said, snuggling up close to me. "Is there anything about you that's not exactly as it seems?"

"Well, let's see. Most people think of me as a pushover, but I can get rowdy. So don't try any slick stuff," I said as I wrapped my arms around her.

"Please. You're nothing but a big old teddy bear."

"Okay. Well a lot of people see me and automatically think I run around with all these different women. But the truth of that matter is . . . I'm a one-woman man."

ACKNOWLEDGMENTS

Never in my wildest dreams did I think I'd be sitting here at four in the morning typing "Thank you's" for my fourth novel. But here I am and I have so many people to thank, but due to space constraints and the Boogie Man at Random House, I have limited time. So let me start with God, thank You. Rashaad Hunter, you are my everything and I love you more and more each day. Linda Hunter, thanks for being the best Mom a guy could ask for. A book just isn't complete without me thanking my family. First up are my wonderful aunts. Aunt Carolyn B.H. Rogers, you are the best. Aunt Carrie Mae Moses, I can always count on you for that winning smile. Aunt Niece, I still miss you.

Uncle Dick, you are the man. Uncle Freddie Rogers, my potna for life.

My dad Louis Johnson, thanks for all those late-night chats. My uncle Clifton Johnson, I will not miss my next dental cleaning. My cousins, who are like brothers to me. Barry, Ann and David, Sharon and Chris, Ray, Lynette, Gervane, Amado and Hunter. Daryl, Anthony and Keith Charles. Uncle Junior. Monica Thaxton and the Thaxtons in Cincinnati, Ohio. Daphne Morrison, Schnell Martin, Tammy Martin and my man Michael J.A. Lewis of the Atlanta P.D.

My entire literary family. Elaine Koster, thanks for handling all of my business. My potna in crime, Eric Jerome Dickey: Keep knocking out those bestsellers, brah. Carl Weber, Gloria Mallette, Mary Morrison, Jihad, your time is coming. Pearl Cleage, such a class act. Kim and Will

ACKNOWLEDGMENTS

Roby, Cameka Spencer, Lolita Files, Victoria Murray, Mary and Willlard Jones, Pam and Rufus Williams, thanks for everything. Melody Guy, you are such a jewel. Danielle Durkin, you're a gem as well. Thanks.

Thanks to all the book clubs and friends who have supported me from day one.

I have too many friends to name, so let me just say thank you to all of you who have supported me throughout.

ABOUT THE AUTHOR

Travis Hunter is the author of the bestsellers *The Hearts of Men, Married but Still Looking,* and *Trouble Man.* He is a motivational speaker and the founder of The Hearts of Men Foundation, through which he mentors under-privileged children. In 2003, he was voted Author of the Year by readers of the *Atlanta Daily World.* For more about Travis Hunter, his books, his tour events, and other news, visit his website at www.travishunter.com.